# Human Slices

22-BOWM

# Human Slices

GLORIA BOWMAN

| Library of Congress Number: | | 00-192562 |
| --- | --- | --- |
| ISBN #: | Hardcover | 0-7388-4446-2 |
| | Softcover | 0-7388-4447-0 |

To order additional copies of this book, contact:
Xlibris Corporation
1-888-7-XLIBRIS
www.Xlibris.com
Orders@Xlibris.com

# Dedication

To women who have chosen to be child free.

# I

Easily alone, completely alone, and very much content being that way, a woman trudged, then sprang, then trudged once again up the granite steps that led to Chicago's Museum of Science & Industry. Coming down the stairs toward her were two young mothers tangled up in strollers, tote bags, and four golden-haired toddlers. The two mothers smiled at the solitary woman in a strange, remorseful way. Did they pity her because she didn't have her own beautiful children? Or could they be a bit jealous, wishing momentarily that they too could be alone and so unburdened? The woman smiled back at the mothers and charged up the last three stairs.

At the museum entrance, she pulled hard to open one of the massive bronze doors. This act was always exciting for as soon as the door would open, for just a second or two, the main hall of the museum appeared to be a fabulous canvas of invention–the bi-planes hanging from the ceiling, the rows of black locomotives, the giant spinning globe. And then, the museum's main hall passed from grandness (how quickly) to being a large, worn, and weirdly contrived series of displays that, upon closer inspection, were dusty, chipped, and dated.

The woman just entering the museum, however, was anything but dusty, chipped, and dated. In her thirties, tall and attractive, she carried herself with impeccable posture. Walking straight made her feel as if all was in good order. She wore a straw hat, with her very dark brown hair tucked neatly inside. "Never let your hair interfere with the design of your chapeau," her Aunt Elaine had always told her. She wore sandals that showed off her toes, the toenails painted a deep red. Her lips were painted a red even darker. She wore a man's white shirt and draping black pants. At first glance, very feminine. At second, potentially androgynous.

On automatic pilot, she headed for the space exploration exhibit. It was there she could always find what she was looking for, a living remnant from her childhood and a long-time friend of the family–a certain museum security guard.

When she saw him, she reached out to pat his shoulder. "Nice to see you, Mr. Johnson," she said, smiling, deepening the tiny beginnings of crow's feet around her eyes.

The guard winked at her, and in a half-hearted salute, he lightly touched the vinyl brim of his hat. "Nice to see you, too, Little Salmon." They fastened onto each other in a warm hug. Little Salmon. She knew that once Mr. Johnson was gone, no one would ever call her that silly nickname so spontaneously and sweetly again. Her mother might use it periodically–but only in a contrived, pointed way, as in "When are you going to start spawning, Little Salmon? You're not getting any younger, you know."

She always wanted to say, "Never, Mother," but was unable to confess such an intention. Instead, she would laugh and shake her head, giving an elusive answer like, "I'm always swimming up river, Mom."

Her father had nicknamed her Little Salmon. He caught a coho salmon the morning she was born. "You were just about as pink and squirmy as that old fish was," he had told her, tickling her belly. "Besides, Little Salmon is a helluva better name than Samantha."

Samantha, of course, was her mother's choice, and it was still her name on ragged-edged documents of birth and baptism, on old report cards and diplomas. Early on, the name Samantha was shortened to Sam. But in college, she began spelling Sam with an *l*. S-A-L-M. It was a tribute to her father and her former pink and squirmy self. "But the *l* is silent," she would say.

After she and Mr. Johnson pulled away from their embrace, he grabbed her shoulders and looked kindly into her eyes. "Helen and me will be lighting a candle for your dad at church this week."

"Thanks, Mr. Johnson," Salm replied. "It's already twenty years," she said.

The guard shook his head. "Unbelievable where the time goes."

Salm squeezed her cheek against his. "Give your wife my best."

"Will do." He saluted her again as she turned to leave. They never said much more than a few words on her annual visit to the museum. It was enough that he was always there for her.

Salm wondered if her mother, who was now remarried and living in Arizona, would mark the day of her first husband's death with any special remembrance. Probably not. She had always avoided such activity. It was her own method of denial.

Salm could remember spending sad adolescent nights alone in her room after her father died. She would lie very still, listening to the muffled sounds of her mother's sobs mingling with the voices of the nightly news. Salm knew her mother wept for her husband and for his premature death. Salm also understood that her mother was crying for herself, a young woman facing life as a widow, angry with her husband leaving her to raise a child alone. Salm sometimes felt abandoned and scared and was afraid that one night her mother would sadly confess, "If I could have chosen losing only one of you, I would have asked God to spare his life and take yours." Back then, Salm sometimes actually wished that that was what would happen— that she could take her father's place. That's how much she knew her mother missed him, and how much Salm wanted to make things right.

But Salm knew her mother wept for her too. "Oh, baby," she would say, holding her daughter tightly, "I hope you never forget the way he looked at you, the way you could light up his eyes, really light up his eyes."

Tears came for different reasons, contradictory and complex, as complicated and muddled as most things in our lives.

Now Salm felt her own tears well up. She recalled her father's image, so out-of-reach tall and swashbuckling handsome in his own guard uniform. He once patrolled these same museum passageways for lost children and destructive teenagers.

When Salm was out of grammar school for summer vacations, she used to bring her father lunch–peanut butter and jelly sandwiches on soft white bread. He would ooh and aah, and the other guards, especially Mr. Johnson, would tousle her hair and pinch her cheeks. She would run from their rough touch to spend the hot summer days roaming the halls of the museum, defiantly leaving her fingerprints on every display case.

Today, she walked through the museum slowly, still leaving fingerprints (that was essential), while wandering along the familiar route of her pilgrimage. There would be the claustrophobic tour of the U-505 German submarine, followed by a look at the extravagant rooms of the gilded dollhouse. Sometimes, if the lines weren't too long, she would take the rough ride down the elevator shaft to the simulated coal mine and then treat herself to a glimpse of the oddly fascinating side-by-side demonstrations of indoor plumbing and "Your Postal Service at Work."

But more than anything else, she was especially fond of the human slices exhibit. That's what she really came for. Salm shivered in anticipation when the slices, sandwiched in glass display cases, came into view.

Out of respect for the two mutilated bodies, a man and a woman, both unidentified corpses from the city morgue, she took time to view the cutaway sections of the foot, the thigh, and the brain, but she preferred the full vertical torso slice of the man. She was intrigued by the expanse of shriveled up liver, the dried crust of pubic hair, and the way the leathery brown skin had separated from the muscle and fat.

Salm thought of her father. By now, nothing much was left of him, and Salm was gloomily comforted by the thought of his decay. Right after he died, she had recurring nightmares of his body being prepared for exhibition on the museum wall. How easily the masked surgeon glided the band saw through the flesh and organs, each human steak falling limply onto the cold steel operating table. Slice by slice. Slab by slab. How relieved she felt when his body, no longer a potential exhibit piece, was lowered into its grave.

Standing at her favorite slice, Salm kneaded the skin on her face and felt the hollows of her eye sockets. She pushed on her cheekbones and sought out an impression of her skull. As often as she examined this exhibit, she could never quite accept the fact that all of the pieces fit together to make two human beings, real bodies. They were chunks of flesh that once walked and talked–real people who once wept and laughed. At one time, the amputated limbs danced. The shriveled organs had beat, breathed, purified, and digested.

Now that the bodies were reduced to nothing but the physical and morbid, Salm pitied them. She pitied herself, too, because the same layers, textures, and shapes were neatly packed inside her own body, waiting for their inevitable doom.

One of her earliest memories was sitting on the museum steps right here at the human slices exhibit, her big-ruled notebook paper in her lap, endlessly sketching and resketching the individual organs and the details of withered flesh. Now, she made her living as a medical illustrator–a specialist in glands, veins, and tendons, not to mention the diseases, viruses, and cancers.

Her Aunt Elaine had funded art school and the additional technical coursework Salm needed for the medical profession. "You've got a talent, Salm. And I've run out of things to spend my money on." Salm's mother thought her daughter's fascination with the human body and its pathologies morbid, but Aunt Elaine used to defend her. "Salm has the wonderful luxury of making her own choices, dear sister. Just let her."

At the human slices exhibit, each rectangular display case jutted out from the wall so that people could observe the slices from both sides. Salm stooped down to examine a shrunken, yellowed stomach from one side of the display case. Playfully, she closed one eye and peered through an open gap between the stomach and the intestines. Through this tiny opening, she could look out to the hallway. She looked left and then right, and then she saw a man appear from around the corner.

He was a prime specimen of that kind of tall, rail thin but strong type of man. His expression, somewhat sullen. His hair, a little long. She stayed still, keeping her eye pushed against the glass and imagining how it must look gazing out from the other side, a blinking eyeball suspended in the decayed ruins of human entrails.

The man spotted her solitary eye staring out at him through the opening in the dried digestive tract. Her staring eye looked gruesome and weird to him. Understandably, he quickly spun around and walked away.

# II

With a slight smile on her face, Salm rounded the staircase that led to the third floor of the museum. There was the man from the human slices again. He was bent over the stairwell, gazing down. Salm knew what he was watching. The open stairwell had a pendulum suspended in it. You could look down all the way to the basement and watch the steel globe move round and around, swinging slowly and methodically, marking the movement of the planet. Salm moved back against the wall to watch him watch the pendulum.

Chance meetings always played a sublime role in her mind's private erotica, and not only had Fate brought him to her at the human slices exhibit, Fate also saw to it that they shared tastes in other things. Salm loved the pendulum too. She had once been so enchanted with it that she built one. For her effort, and with the help of her father, she took a first place science prize in third grade.

The man leaned a little more over the railing. Then a little more. Maybe too far. It seemed a bit dangerously too far. Then Salm heard a voice come out of nowhere. "Hey! Hey! You! You, buddy!" It was a guard—a young, greasy looking fellow. He yanked at the man's leg. "What the hell you think you're doin'? You tryin' to kill yourself or something?"

The man looked at the guard with stunned disbelief. "Sorry," he said, shrugging.

"Get out of here," the guard growled.

Salm, feeling uncomfortable and embarrassed for staring, turned toward the steps to leave.

As she ascended the stairs, she sensed he was following behind her. She felt the pulse of some invisible electrical current running from her body back toward his. She was certain he wasn't following her on purpose (and she was right). He was simply going in the same direction. She continued walking, periodically monitoring his presence by turning her head, pretending she was stretching a sore neck or checking the whereabouts of an imaginary companion. She felt her underarms and the small of her back going clammy.

With him still behind her, Salm headed for the reproductive display, the highlight of which was a row of human fetuses, once alive, now tucked into a series of black velvet cases, tracing the nine months of physical development from speck-sized inception to full-grown infant.

The man followed her through the slow-moving line as they took in the eerie sight of the pickled unborn. They were beautiful things, those fetuses. The distended curvature of the miniature skulls, the yellow translucence of the curled up bodies, and that veil of angel hair that stuck to semi-identifiable parts of the alien creatures—all of it appealed to Salm. She stared at their eyes, their tiny, clenched fingers, their fragile and fearful postures.

Seeing the fetuses always made Salm appreciate the miracle and the phantasm of childbirth. And it always made her wonder why she felt so absolutely sure that she never wanted to experience it. Was it the weight of responsibility of having a child? The sheer oddity of carrying a life form inside her own body? Was it some rebellious need to defy natural and social order? She had never come up with the answer. She had never made an intellectual decision to be childless—or child free, depending on one's perspective. She just knew it was what she wanted.

Once, she had confided to her Aunt Elaine her total lack of interest in creating a human being. Aunt Elaine had responded, "No particular doom will befall you if you choose not to have children, Salm."

"But I wonder sometimes," Salm replied, "if something is wrong with me. I have absolutely no desire to reproduce. None. At all. Not a fleeting moment of it. Ever."

"You're not alone," Aunt Elaine whispered while she looked around furtively. "There are women like you everywhere. They just don't talk about it. It's too risky."

"Risky?" Salm asked.

"If you say you don't want children, you know what people think of you? They'll think you're nearly evil. Frigid. Selfish. Unnatural. So you have to get by just knowing you're not alone and that the myth about maternal instinct doesn't ring true for everyone."

Salm remembered feeling amazed by her aunt's words. Were there really a lot of other women like her?

She had forgotten about the stranger behind her until she felt a tug at her shirt. She turned abruptly.

"Excuse me," he said. "Do you have any change?" Salm didn't respond. She was stunned.

"Really. I mean it," he said. "Got any change?" He looked down at the bag that hung from her shoulder. "For the vending machines. I just realized I didn't bring any change, and I need some for the vending machines."

Salm smiled at him. She understood. A visit to the museum wasn't complete unless you bought something from one of those machines, so she shrugged her purse off her shoulder and reached down into the bottom, pulling out a handful of coins and loose tobacco. Some of the coins were coated with chips of dried green gum. She held out her hand to him, and he picked out two quarters, two of the clean quarters, that is. He was careful not to touch Salm's little finger, a shriveled and small specimen, a defect from birth.

She ignored his reaction to her minor deformity. Her father always told her that the tiny finger made her special, and she believed it was true.

"The vending machines aren't on this floor," Salm said. "They're in the basement."

"I know," the man said. He held the change tightly and raised his fist in a gesture of appreciation. "Thanks."

Now it was her turn to follow. She kept a five-foot distance behind him as they passed the walk-through heart, its loud beating sending deep tremors through the concrete floor.

When they got to the lower level of the museum, he stopped short in front of the vending machines. Salm disappeared into the bathroom.

# III

The man stood at the vending machine stocked with novelty toys–things like key chains, whistles, mirrors, and magic tricks. For a few minutes he just stared at the tiny treasures wondering why he found them all so appealing.

He felt connected to everything in the museum–the exhibits, the pillars, the heavy bronze doors. He always thought it odd that a museum dedicated to the workings of science and industry could provoke such a personal response in him, much more than any fine art collection could, and he felt a slight memory of anger thinking about the time he worked there. He had worked at the museum once for a day, or rather, a few hours.

He remembered being happy with the maintenance job, especially when he found out that one of his nightly tasks would be cleaning the chicken incubator. Right before he got started, he knelt down to be eye level with an egg, one that was rocking ever so slightly, with an anticipatory twitch. He waited and waited. Finally, a tiny yellow beak poked through the shell. At that moment, a supervisor came up behind him. "You the new guy?" he asked.

"Yeah."

The supervisor noted the plastic name badge clipped onto the pocket of his uniform. It said, in simple type, 'Luke.' "You're supposed to be cleaning this place, Luke, not playing science experiment."

"Yeah. OK," Luke answered. "I'll get to it. Right after the chicken hatches."

"Well, that's not what you're paid to do around here." The supervisor stood tall and crossed his arms over his broad chest.

"Then don't pay me." And as Luke turned to leave, to punch his timecard and turn in his blue work uniform, the pink flesh of the chicken's head, covered with wet, spiked hair, miraculously pushed through the membrane.

Even now, Luke could remember the birth of that chicken as vividly as he could remember anything. He could also imagine its death, its neck wrenched, its plucked body shrink-wrapped for the freezer section, ready to be selected and consumed at some suburban barbecue.

Luke shook his head and the image of the chicken was erased.

His was still staring at the toys in the vending machine when Salm walked out of the bathroom, wiping her wet hands on the seat of her pants. She hated using those blow dryers and the paper towel supply was depleted.

She stopped and stood next to him. "You don't have too many choices, you know. The selection in these machines hasn't changed for about a gazillion years."

Luke cocked his head, taken aback by her appearance. "Yeah, but you can always count on this stuff to be here, just like it's supposed to be. They're constants."

He inserted the fifty cents he had "borrowed" from her and pulled at the round knob below the plastic schnauzers, two black and white miniature dogs whose magnetic bases were designed to make them jerk and dance and frolic with each other when they were placed on a metal surface.

"I have some of those," Salm said as she watched him open the box.

"Me too," he answered. "Lots of 'em." He laid the dogs in his hand.

"Constant or not, they're not very good magnets." Salm took the toys out of his hand and placed them on the side of the vending machine. They slid down, moving toward each other, then apart, until they finally broke contact and fell to the floor. Salm laughed. "See. They're lousy."

Luke shrugged, bent over to pick up the magnets, and pushed them into his front pants pocket. "But, you know what?" he asked, smiling, his eyes glistening.

"What?"

"They stick good enough."

# IV

Salm, alone, lay on her back in bed that night thinking about the time that had passed since her father died. She tried to remember every Christmas with him, but could not. As she stared at the darkness of the ceiling, one of her cats kneaded at her breast, and then leisurely walked up and down the length of her body until it finally settled down on her pelvis, the cat's favorite resting spot.

Salm slightly winced when the cat's weight pressed down on her. She sometimes had that little pain when she was ovulating. She made a mental note to make an appointment with her gynecologist.

She thought about her doctor briefly. It was no simple task to find one who so easily accepted a patient who said, "I don't want to have children. Never have and never will." Other gynecologists had looked at her with disdain when she explained how she felt. Some had told her, "Oh, you'll change your mind when the right guy comes along." Or, "You'll get over being that selfish." Or, "Having a child is why you're put here on earth. You'll want one one day."

But this doctor had said to Salm, "Sure, I've heard that before. Some women never do want to have kids. There's no rule that says you have to." Salm remembered the words so clearly. "It could very well be that you have, say, a tipped uterus or some kind of ovulation dysfunction. Matter over mind, you know. It's often the case."

Salm had pondered that idea for years. What if that were the case? What if, because she had something malformed or malfunctioning inside of her, her subconscious had been sending her a subliminal message for years? It would have repeated over and over: "You will not want children. You will not want children." Could there have been some sort of psychological protection system set up in her head so that she wouldn't be devastated when she discovered she was unable to reproduce?

She supposed it was possible. She liked the idea of something being physically wrong with her. It was the best excuse. So when someone rudely asked, "No children yet?"

Salm could say, "I can't," and pretend to be burdened.

"Oh," the world would whisper. "Poor dear."

(Salm had been asked many times by many people, sometimes even strangers, why she wasn't yet a mother, and it annoyed her that these same people would never feel equally compelled to ask a new parent: "So . . . why did you decide to have that child?")

The cat got up and walked in circles around Salm's pelvis. She lay still, posing questions to herself: Why do cats instinctively walk round and round in circles? Why can't I stop thinking about that man from the museum? Why do I have to validate my choice not to have children?

Another of her cats joined Salm in bed. Purring, it ceremoniously burrowed its head into her hair, licking her scalp, and chewing on her hair. "Night, Peanut," Salm whispered. She stroked the animal until it, and she, fell to sleep. Salm slept soundly. She always did.

# V

Unlike Salm, Luke never slept for more than a few hours at once. He merely napped. Morning, afternoon, early evening.

While Salm breathed the deep breaths of sleep, while her darting eyes followed the movement of some fantastic dream, Luke woke up with a jolt at five in the morning. After a quick shower, he pulled on his clothes, and in minutes he was ready to face the day. He opened the heavy door to his storefront apartment and collapsed the wrought iron gate that slouched across the entranceway. Standing at the open door, he swallowed deep breaths of cool spring air, exhaling clouds of purplish gray. He pulled the door and gate closed and strolled down the street. Head down, he watched the sidewalk move beneath him. It was cracked and broken. Pieces of asphalt jutted up and down as if some kind of earth tremor repositioned each slab.

He usually walked every morning regardless of the time he awakened—not for health reasons—but because there was nothing more he enjoyed than the act of plain old looking around.

He simply went where his legs would take him, and his mind followed. Together they would explore all over the city. Looking. Thinking. From the grandest buildings to the decaying ones, he could spend time examining their stones and bricks, wood and glass. He was intrigued by details, images, and textures—a craggy tree limb growing through a fence, an ant struggling with an oversized crumb, a crumpled piece of paper floating in a muddy puddle. He was a dedicated thing-watcher, not a people-watcher. People watching required a different type of focus.

On West Fullerton, he stopped to look into the window of a currency exchange. The skeletal reflection of his drawn face reminded him of someone. He saw the reflection of his eye. That woman from the museum. He knew he had seen her before, and he tried to remember from where. Then suddenly, down a nearby alley, he heard the roar and crash of a garbage truck, and any thought of her went right into the dumpster inside his own brain. It was easy for him to dismiss thoughts that required energy he didn't want to expend.

Luke continued walking as if pulled by a string, a string that connected him to the city somehow. Sometimes he would walk a block, sometimes miles.

This morning, he had awakened after a bout with his recurring nightmare, the one where his right leg is twisted off by a giant spool in a textile mill. The dream always began the same. He would be alone, walking through this factory, and an oversized bobbin would catch his foot, and the roaring machine would rip his leg from his pelvis. He would lie on the floor, screaming and writhing in pain, watching his leg spin into the thread, disappearing under layers and layers of demonic string.

Just in case this nightmare predicted a reality, Luke kept an artificial leg hanging in his back room. He was relieved by the presence of the slick, plastic flesh. It was important to him to be prepared for tragedies, even though the tragedies he prepared for never came.

His one true friend in the world, George, taught at their alma mater, the Art Institute of Chicago. George had always laughingly promised to make Luke a see-through plastic leg that could double as an aquarium. "That way," he had told Luke, "the artificial leg would at least be practical to have around until you need it."

# VI

Salm rarely woke up early unless a car alarm, barking dogs, or police sirens shook her from sleep. This morning, it was the telephone that brought her to life. Her three faithful girlfriends were confirming their meeting at "The Cup" for breakfast. Although their 10:00 am Saturday morning date had stood for years, they still called each other as a reminder. These were women who didn't trust commitments of any kind, even among friends. Alien forces—like hangovers, lovers, unexpected diversions, or just plain laziness—often prohibited perfect attendance for this (sort of) weekly ritual. But today, they all were going to be there.

When Salm arrived at the neighborhood diner, Sylvia, Wendy, and Claire already had the booth fortified with two pots of coffee. With a feeble morning nod, Salm slid in next to Claire and poured herself a cup of steaming caffeine. Then she lit a cigarette with Wendy's lighter, a lighter she examined carefully. It looked suspiciously like the one she lost last week. All four of the women were reformed smokers, except when they were together. Then, they were excessive about whatever it was they were consuming—tobacco, coffee, chocolate, each other's sex stories, alcohol. It was tradition. "Like college," Wendy always rationalized.

They came to this diner because they could sit for hours, the coffee supply was unlimited, and no one ever asked them to extinguish a cigarette. Nearly every table always had its own stinky gray cloud hovering overhead.

Claire filled Salm in on the conversation. "We were talking about this article I read," she said.

"About what?" asked Salm.

"Mate selection."

"Spare me." Salm gulped down her first coffee of the day as Nick, the owner of the restaurant, approached their table.

"How are all of my beauties this morning?" The women smiled and nodded. Salm nestled under the thick arm that Nick curled around her shoulder. He called all of his regular female customers "beauties." When he became a grandfather for the first time, everyone kidded him that he should have his son name the baby Beauty so grandpa wouldn't forget her name.

"You didn't order yet?" he asked, raising a bushy eyebrow. He looked around and shot a glare at the waitress as she flew by, balancing four platters on her right arm.

"Be right there!" She sang the words happily, seeming to enjoy her work.

"Oh, no, no. Don't hassle the waitress, Nick," Wendy butted in. "We haven't been waiting long. Besides, we were waiting for Salm before we ordered."

Nick wagged a reprimanding finger at Salm and walked away. Everyone knew she was perpetually late for everything.

Claire continued as if there had been no interruption. "So in this article, they're making this grand assumption."

"Who's they?"

"The magazine. I don't know which one. I was looking over a woman's shoulder on the subway. Some women's magazine, or girl magazine, I guess."

"And the grand assumption is?" Salm asked.

"That everyone—every woman, that is—wants the same thing. You know. A husband, a family. According to this article, by the time you're 21 or something, you should be heavily into your search for a 'life partner.' Like what kind of p.c. phrase is that for husband-chasing? But the article never said anything about charting your own course, you know. Giving some guiding words about taking your time, exploring the options. It was just, I don't know, the article was setting up young women to be so desperate or something."

"Women in general can set themselves up to feel desperate," added Sylvia, "without the help of any article."

"Yeah, but the worst part was there were these tips about designing a selection process, like you're shopping for a car or buying a horse."

"Isn't that how it's always worked—for both sides?"

"No kidding." Claire gulped her coffee. "But this how-to crap in this article, was so . . . so confining, I don't know, so limiting. It was saying to make a list of x amount of attributes and go out and get someone to fit exactly what you're looking for. Like how do you really know when you're young? Or how do you *ever* know for that matter?"

Their favorite waitress, the one with the pointed teeth and horrible scars on her forearms, took their breakfast orders—one jalapeño omelet, two scrambled with bacon, two basted with sausage, and french toast without the powdered sugar.

Salm openly stared at the waitress's scars. She had told her once that she had some tattoos removed.

When the ordering was done, Claire continued. "Like what kind of bullshit advice is that? I mean, the best part has always been the chase and the unknown, right? Making it a job, I mean, what fun is that? The fun part is the not knowing."

"Sometimes, I suppose," Sylvia answered. Wendy and Salm exchanged looks.

"For instance," Claire said, "let's say it's not on your list that your future mate needs to be involved in what? Politics? You never gave a rat's ass about politics. But you meet a guy who does. What happens? Omit him from your life? Cross him off because he's into something that's not on your pre-qualifications list? That's what this advice column was saying. But what if you don't cross him off? What if he introduces you to this new politics thing, and you find out that you could get really into it, and there you go, you're running for alderman in a couple of years and maybe you'll do something to make the world better. That's what's key—keeping open to the possibilities."

"Nobody's arguing with you, Claire," Salm said. "Of course it's stupid to limit your choices when there are a lot of great men out there."

"There are?" Wendy asked. After years of seeking (and failing to find) the right mate, Wendy had been artificially inseminated. Once she gave birth, she decided that the only male who would ever interest her again would be her son, Matthew.

"There *are* a lot of good guys out there," Claire said. "But you have to be willing to give them a chance. How else are you going to discover what you really want?"

"I know what I want," Wendy said, "and that's zero involvement with any man."

Claire laughed. "But you're an aberration."

"Me? An aberration?" She looked at each of her friends. "And the other people at this table?" All of the women smiled back at her.

Claire was known for her obsessive pursuit of lust and love—never satisfied, always searching for romance and passion. She wanted to live the text of bodice-ripping novels, and oftentimes did. Sylvia had a "life partner," her live-in boyfriend Armando, whom she didn't even like.

"And then there's Salm," Sylvia said, "the one who seeks attachment and then flees from it when it's offered. How many times have you almost gotten married now?"

Salm shrugged. "I don't know. Ten, eleven, twelve." She had, indeed, been proposed to four times. And, with an incredible primal fear shining in her eyes, she said "yes" to every one because she felt obligated and didn't want to hurt anyone's feelings. But she always knew rejection would follow when the topic of children arose. When she would get around to saying, "I don't want any," the engagement would soon be be null and void.

The waitress arrived with platters of food and side dishes of toast and hash browns, and the women arranged and rearranged the plates and cups and ashtrays as if playing some elaborate, well-rehearsed shell game. Finally, they were situated. They began to eat, stuffing big forkfuls into their mouths, forgetting anything they ever knew about table manners. They could do that sort of thing with one another.

Salm spoke with her mouth full of eggs and hot sauce. "So what'd you do last night, Syl?"

"Developed a strategy for life partnering," Sylvia deadpanned. The women rolled their eyes in unison and went back to their food.

There was a sudden draft and Salm looked toward the diner's front door. Of all the people in the world, the man from the museum walked in and grabbed a stack of newspapers near the coat rack. Salm immediately put her fork down and wiped hot sauce from her chin.

She was engulfed by grand fantasies about chance meetings and love and romance being predestined by the stars. Her life and his were being drawn together for some reason at this small moment in this same room. It was exciting to her. It was magical, and she suddenly felt charged.

Luke took a table for two across from the booth where Salm and her friends sat. He didn't notice them. And even though Salm tried not to be obvious, her friends quickly realized that she was watching someone.

"Who are you looking at?" Sylvia whispered.

"Nobody." Salm was embarrassed. They were all adults, and they should know how to behave in public. But Salm knew her friends too well. As soon as she would point out the object of her attention, they would abruptly crane their necks and stare.

Claire looked around and jerked her head toward Luke. "It's him, isn't it?" She knew Salm's type—the thin, the somewhat unsettling, the rarity. Ever since college, Claire and Salm were never competitive about potential lovers. Claire adored the manly, gregarious type. Salm was taken by the withdrawn and mysterious.

Finally, sensing being watched, Luke looked up toward the women's table. Salm's eyes caught his glance so she lifted her coffee mug to her lips and toasted him. He nodded slightly and looked back to his paper.

The women continued eating, and Salm's attention quietly went back to the stranger. She couldn't help herself. She was being guided solely by her insides, and she almost always respected the course they chose.

She nonchalantly watched him, hoping to get his attention again. But he never looked up at her, and she just kept watching. She watched him eat a corned beef sandwich. After he pushed his plate away, she listened to him ask for more coffee. Then she watched him look for something. He patted his shirt pockets, then his jacket. He extended his right leg and dug into the front pocket of his black jeans. She smiled as he pulled out the two magnetic schnauzers he bought at the museum. He seemed surprised to find them in his pocket and laid them on the table. She heard him ask the waitress for matches. She watched him smoke and drink coffee. She watched him read the newspaper. Everything he did was fascinating to her.

She noted that he earnestly scanned the classifieds. No job? New job? She wondered what he did. He didn't even glance at the sports section. She thought that was an exceptional sign.

When it was almost noon, the women got up from their table and collected their possessions. As they slipped on light jackets and sweaters, Salm couldn't help herself. She felt an uncontrollable urge and took three big steps that put her right next to his table.

She smiled, a little too flirtatiously, and hated herself for being so bold but at the same time gave herself credit for such boldness. "Got any change?" she asked him.

"Change? What for?" he asked.

She pointed at the dog magnets lying on his table.

"Oh, so if I don't pay you back, you're going to repossess them?" he said, charming her completely.

Claire, Wendy, and Sylvia went to the cash register to pay the bill. They tried to inconspicuously watch the unfolding interaction.

Luke placed the two dogs into his palm. His fingers were bony and long, and his life line curved down his hand to the y-shaped vein at the inside of his wrist. He offered the dogs up to her.

She took them and pasted them onto the chrome-topped sugar container. The little things barely hung on, jerking and sliding down the smooth surface.

"Like I said then, they don't stick too well," Salm observed.

"But they *are* magical," he said, sending her a flash of electric current with his eyes.

Salm just stood there, staring at the dogs. She couldn't think of anything else to say. "See ya," was all there was. He raised his eyebrows at her in surprise, and she left the side of his table to join her friends who were standing at the front door of the restaurant.

Outside the diner, the women discussed the day's plans. They didn't ask about Salm's conversation with the stranger. There was something in her frozen expression that said, "Don't even ask me what I just did." She felt dazed. Why did she walk away? What was wrong with her?

Claire said she was going to the grocery store. "Maybe I'll meet the man of my dreams in the imported cheese section and I won't have to go to Greece this summer." Sylvia said she was going home to break up with Armando, but no one believed her.

Wendy, as usual, was in a hurry. She had to go to her mother's and pick up her baby. She tried not to rely on her mother too much for babysitting so she could spare herself the lectures about her selfishness and the tragedy of single motherhood and about how her-mother-never-had-any-free-babysitting-when-her-kids-were-growing-up.

Salm would merely think about doing her laundry, but wouldn't be able to motivate herself. Later in the afternoon, she would go to a matinee. One of her favorite movies of all time was playing at the Music Box Theater.

# VII

Salm spoke quietly to the beautiful queen manning the ticket booth. "Just one please."

She enjoyed most solitary afternoon activity, but there was something conspicuous about being alone at the movies. She always thought that people alone at matinees looked like perverts, including herself. She hated that kind of paranoid feeling and knew it well. It was the same feeling that drove her to ask for not one, but two sodas, when she ordered out for a pizza late at night. "I'll get it!" she would yell to an invisible stranger while she opened the front door ever so slightly. She wouldn't want the delivery man to think she was some kind of tragic lonely heart waiting to act out a scene from a porn movie. Sometimes, being alone was OK. Sometimes it wasn't.

As she left the ticket counter, she heard a familiar male voice behind her. "One please," it said. Her internal radar system went on full alert. It just could not be that the man from the museum had followed her. Could Fate be that determined? Was it possible that they could have ended up at the same place three times in a mere twenty-four hours? She didn't dare turn around for fear of being disappointed when he wasn't there.

At the concession stand, she ordered popcorn and poured a load of finely ground salt into the greasy box. The man behind her tugged at her jacket. When Salm turned and saw it was him, she felt her stomach first twitch, then flutter, and finally convulse. She counted. One-two-three-four. She had to catch her breath. She could not risk hyperventilating and maybe passing out. Then she was struck with an irrational fear that he was afraid *she* was following him. What if he thought she was a stalker? "But wait a minute!" she argued with herself. "I was here first."

"Are you OK?" he asked. "You look a little . . ." He didn't know how she looked, but he knew she didn't look comfortable.

Salm took a deep breath. "Yeah. I'm fine. I was just surprised. Surprised to see you."

"You know," he said, "when we talked at the museum, I thought I knew you from somewhere, and I just realized how we first met."

"You know me?" she asked. "We met before?" She was still counting. Eleven . . . twelve . . . thirteen. She could barely look at him. She was feeling silly and giddy, and she liked it.

He stood at the candy counter and pointed to a box of caramels. He turned back to Salm. "Yeah. We did meet before. We had a little accident."

"We did?"

"Remember? I was a messenger once, for City Express."

On the impact of his words, her brain delivered a clear image of a bad memory. "Oh, no. You were the guy on the bicycle?"

"Yeah, that was me."

Salm tossed her head and faked a laugh. "So that was you." She remembered running across Lake Street one afternoon, trying to make an elevated train, when a bicycle delivery man came out of nowhere from around the corner. She jumped out of the way. He swerved, trying to avoid an accident, but caught his handlebar in the strap of her bag. He grabbed onto her arm to stop them both from falling and they spun around, knitting the bicycle, their bodies, and bags together. "You OK?" he had asked, as they detangled themselves. "You OK?" he asked again. She remembered not being able to respond. Everything had happened so quickly, yet at the same time, it seemed as if it had happened in slow motion. She knew she wasn't hurt, but she remembered not being able to respond. Readjusted on his seat, the bike man pushed his delivery bag back onto his shoulder, and sped off, not saying he was sorry. She had memorized his identification number.

"So that was you," Salm repeated.

"Yup."

She took a breath. "I'll confess. I called the company to complain," she said.

"I know. I lost my job." He smiled at her, and Salm was embarrassed by her past anger. She hadn't tried to get him fired. A reprimand would have been enough.

Suddenly realizing that people got shot over situations like this, Salm spun around to make her way down the aisle of the old movie house as she anxiously shoved popcorn into her mouth. She took a seat in the third row, fourth seat in.

Luke stood at the leather doors at the back of the theater and watched her. He was glad she liked sitting up front. It didn't even cross his mind that she was a little afraid of him. He interpreted her walking away as an invitation, so his legs carried him to the seat next to her, on her right. He moved his chin close to her shoulder. "Well, thanks a lot for calling," he whispered. "It was my first day on that job."

When he smiled, he became conscious of the taste of menthol cigarettes that lined his mouth and hoped that the smell didn't annoy her.

Intimidated by his invasion of her personal territory, Salm sank into the padded chair and forced her knees up against the back of the seat in front of her. If he started a scene, she could run out to the left. No one else was in their row. Maybe he just wanted an apology, but she vowed to herself not to do that. He had been in the wrong, downright rude. At least he could have said he was sorry.

"My name's Luke," he said. He didn't know what else to say. He certainly wasn't going to apologize for running into her. She shouldn't have been crossing in the middle of the street. He had blown the silver whistle the company gave all of its employees. It wasn't his fault she didn't hear it.

Not sensing her nervousness, Luke let his elbow take control of the armrest between them. Salm inched her body away from his.

"I'm sorry," he said.

"I'm sorry too." She turned and gave him a sickly smile. She was crazy about him and he probably wanted to kill her.

"What's your name again?" he asked.

She didn't respond. He waited.

"Salm," she finally answered, not being able to make up a pseud-onym at a moment's notice.

"Sam?"

"Yeah. But with an *l*." To herself she screamed, "Don't keep talking to this guy!"

"Sam with an *l*?"

"The *l* is silent." She paused. "It's a long story." She paused again. "Look. I didn't mean to get you fired."

"No problem. I should probably thank you." The coming attrac-tions flashed on the screen. After an announcement warning ladies to keep their handbags off the seat next to them, the film, "A Zed and Two Noughts," began.

"You've seen this before?" Luke asked.

Salm nodded, "Yeah. Three times." She rested her head against the curve of the seatback and stared at the theater's midnight blue ceiling, sprinkled with flashing stars. She was no longer afraid that he was going to assault her, but worried that he was the kind of person who would talk through a movie. He wasn't. He simply wanted to know if she had come here by accident, or if she was attached to the film and its soundtrack as much as he was.

Their conversation ended when Luke said, "I've seen it five times." They both stared ahead at the screen. The film was one of Luke's favorites even though he never was able to make sense of the narrative. He loved the images—severely beautiful and haunting renderings of death and love, birth and decay, captivity and freedom. The ending always killed him too. The main characters, Siamese twins, who had been separated at birth but were now living in one giant body suit, commit an elaborate ritual of double suicide, and they record their deaths and ensuing decomposition with time lapse photography.

During the first amputation scene in the movie, Luke offered Salm his box of caramels. She shook her head twice, indicating the negative, but her elbow took the opportunity to push Luke's a little so that they could share the armrest. This quarter inch of physical contact made them both so uncomfortable that neither of them seemed able to breathe, but neither of them would move.

Luke glanced down and compared the size of her deformed little finger to his. There was quite a difference. And there was something about it that looked both unreal and inviting. He was so taken with the shriveled little finger that he thought he might need to touch it. So he did.

# VIII

When the film was over, they both stood and stretched, their bodies aching from sitting so perfectly still for so long. Together, they hesitantly walked up the aisle, each making sure the other was following, wanting to delay their disconnection for as long as possible.

They walked out of the theater, squinting, and waited a moment for their eyes to adjust to the light. Outside the theater, the air glowed with a gaudy intensity. Spring time. Tornado weather. Miles away to the north, dark storm clouds gathered into brooding bunches.

"Want to have a drink?" Luke asked.

Salm looked into his eyes. They were the eyes of someone who could be dangerous to her soul. Regardless, she wanted to go with him.

"Sure," she said. "A drink would be fine." Salm began to keep pace with the rhythm of Luke's long-legged strides.

"Before, in the theater, you said 'Sam with an *I*'?" Luke asked her.

"Short for Salmon. Or for Samantha. One name given by my father. One by my mother."

"It's not always easy pleasing everybody," he responded.

She was glad that he understood that.

They walked down Southport Avenue past old taverns and newly constructed condominiums, junk stores, and trendy boutiques. Luke took the lead, nudging Salm to the right or to the left, down Ashland Avenue with its four lanes of traffic whizzing by, then along the quiet residential streets, meandering, never quite finding the right place for that drink he had offered. They discovered they both lived in Chicago all of their lives and one of their favorite things about it was that it was a good city to walk around in. And so they continued to walk, sometimes choosing not to share words, sometimes sharing memories, little glimpses into their personalities, or just general observations about the world: "I once saw a huge car accident at this intersection." "There were some positive things about wearing braces at age 19." "Now over there, that's a good used record store."

They walked on and on, each step leading them to a newer comfort level. Salm told Luke that she was at the Museum of Science & Industry the day before to mark the anniversary of her father's death. Spontaneously, Luke slung his arm over Salm's shoulder and squeezed it. "I'm sorry," he said. "That's rough." Salm felt as if she would melt from his touch. When he hesitantly withdrew his arm from her shoulder, she felt cold. It was as if their flesh had a distinct need to join forces. As they continued walking, he would touch her arm now and then to punctuate a point in his conversation, and she would do the same to him.

They walked for nearly three hours. Luke seemed genuinely surprised when they ended up in front of his storefront. He hadn't planned to bring her here. It just happened. He stopped, and with a flourish, he pulled open the metal burglar gate and kicked open the door.

"How about that drink?" he asked.

Salm glanced around the entranceway. It was a storefront, yes, but it didn't seem to be a public place anymore.

"Come on in," Luke said.

Salm looked up and down the street and noted where she was. "It seems I've been here before," she said, curious, as she followed Luke inside. Like a marionette, she had given up control. Leg followed leg.

Luke moved ahead of her and turned on a light.

They were standing in a bar. Or what had once been a bar. A stage, flanked by giant speakers, sat to the right of the entrance, and on the stage, a microphone stood alone. Tables and chairs filled the center of the room. Bar stools were pushed up against the bar, and the bar itself was overrun with newspapers and junk mail. Salm stood quietly and continued taking inventory. Another light was switched on and a tent of blue neon illuminated a bevy of mannequins standing in the far corner. The mannequins' arms had been removed, and two of the heads were twisted on backwards. Luke watched the recognition appear in Salm's eyes.

"Ah-ha," she responded. "The L&J. I remember the mannequins."

"Hard to forget my girls."

"I would have remembered if the sign was still up out front. The L&J–I remember those letters in that really grand script."

"Good memory," Luke said, going behind the bar. "I had to take the sign down. People kept thinking I was still open."

Salm climbed onto a bar stool and lit two candles.

"Beer, wine, or bourbon? That's all I stock these days."

She remembered the crowds that had once gathered here. "The L&J," she said again, shaking her head to show a bit of disbelief. "This was a great place." She struggled to recollect a possible interaction with Luke–a hello, a drink, a smile–but nothing came through. She could recall suffering from an incredible crush on a bartender with ravaged skin. She, Sylvia, and Claire had stopped in for drinks many times. It could have been seven or even eight years ago. Longer? Ten years?

Luke drew two dusty glasses from behind the bar. He wiped them clean with his index finger. "So . . . bourbon?"

Salm paused, then nodded. "Sure." She watched him evenly pour the liquor into the glasses. "So . . . you live here?"

Luke nodded while he cleared a place on the bar for their drinks. "Yup. For a long time. I don't even know. Nine years now?"

He was interested in the possibility of their having a previous contact. "You really used to come here?" he asked.

"Yeah." Salm spun around on her bar stool and pressed her back against the curved wooden edge of the bar. Four circular booths, the backs tufted with red vinyl, lined the wall opposite her. The tabletop in one booth was filled with mannequin arms, and another was loaded with rags and tools. The booth in the far corner no longer had a table in it at all. In the place of a tabletop, there was a bed covered with a rumpled mess of pillows, sheets, and blankets.

Luke came out from behind the bar and sat next to Salm.

"I'm trying to remember you," Salm said. "But I can't."

"I was always around."

She shrugged. "Sorry I don't remember."

"I'm not insulted." He looked at her closely. "I don't remember you from back then either."

"I do remember one guy, one with really bad skin. A bartender."

Luke laughed. "That was probably my cousin Greg."

"I used to come in here with my girlfriends, sort of stalking him, I guess."

"You can't do that anymore," Luke said. He paused and looked down at the floor for a moment. "He's dead."

"Oh, no." Salm looked at the floor too.

Luke decided to answer her unspoken question. "He overdosed in the men's room."

Salm felt her heart stop. "I'm sorry," she said.

"Things happen." Luke looked up at her and Salm recognized an earnestness and kindness in his eyes that she hadn't seen before. She didn't want to talk about (or even think about) Greg being dead. We'll explore that later, she thought to herself. So she took a big, big breath and a big swig of bourbon and changed the subject. "So what possessed you to move in here and make it home?" she asked.

He paused and thought for a moment. "I don't know."

"There has to be a reason."

"I guess I always lived here. It was my parents' place, the bar, that is. The L&J. L, Luke, was my dad. J was my Uncle Jerry. We lived upstairs. Mom died. Then dad, then Anne Marie."

"Who's she?"

"Jerry's second wife. Then Jerry. And then there was only me . . . and Greg."

"But live in the bar?"

"It was here."

"That's it?" Salm asked. She hated vague answers to important questions.

"I don't know. Decision by drift? The way we make a lot of decisions in our lives. When we closed up shop, well, when *I* did, Greg was dead by then, it seemed to make sense to move into the bar and rent out the apartment upstairs. That's where I used to live. Upstairs."

"But why did you close it at all? It was a pretty happenin' place." Salm sipped her bourbon and looked again at the bed in the corner. She probably sat in that booth in the past and wondered what it would be like to sleep there now.

"Greg and me–ever since we were kids–we always helped our old men pour beers for the guys in the neighborhood. We thought we could handle being entrepreneurs. And actually, Greg could, and well, me–I couldn't. Without trying, the place got hip, the neighborhood started changing. It got too demanding, like a 24-hour day commitment."

"So that was it?" she asked. "You just closed up?"

"After Greg died. I had no choice really. I couldn't run the bar without him." Luke laughed suddenly. "The junkie was the one holding it together. How's that for one of life's great ironies? I sure as hell couldn't. I don't know if I didn't care, didn't have the attention span, didn't want to be working in the bar all the time. Who knows? I just let the liquor license expire and moved in."

Salm looked at him, feeling herself drawn to him more and more. He was a little unsafe, she could tell. But she liked it. It was a good kind of unsafe. Intriguing. Perplexing. Guaranteed to cause heartbreak and distress, but well worth the effort.

"Anyway," Luke went on, "it seemed stupid just to let the place sit vacant. I wouldn't have sold it or anything. And it didn't seem right to let the business pass into strangers' hands. In fact, I had made this pseudo pledge to my father that I wouldn't. You know? Attachment stuff. There's a generation of ghosts here I feel that I owe. So I have a place to live, and I'm a landlord. My dad and Jerry bought up a few places in the neighborhood years ago. I have tenants upstairs, around the corner, down the street." He mockingly puffed himself up a little. "And I'm a helluva handyman."

She was mesmerized. Not only was he a heartbreaker, he knew how to fix things. For awhile, there was nothing left to say, so they sat in silence. He waited for her to speak, and patiently, she waited for him.

While the faucet behind the bar dripped, Salm's mind replayed thousands of microsecond scenarios in her head, scenes that included rape and torture and sensational headlines. Others had to do with finding true love and frolics in gardens dusted with yellow and orange butterflies. There were practical thoughts floating in her head too. She thought about her Aunt Elaine advising her, "I know you girls do it all the time, but I would highly suggest never, never sleeping with a man on a first date."

"What about sleeping with a man even *before* the first date, Aunt Elaine?" she asked herself.

And she thought about how good the bourbon tasted even though she was never a bourbon drinker before.

Luke's brain was working on a similar wavelength. Was she crazy or rational? Tender or perverted? Would he regret this day or would it be one to remember? He wondered if he still had some condoms in the medicine cabinet. He wondered if the Pirates game was on television. He thought about an amputation scene from the movie. Sometimes, he thought of nothing at all.

And while their minds invented, conceived, and contrived images and ideas, they stared. She at him. He at her. Their eyes were intent on investigating and memorizing the exact shape and detail of each other's forehead, brows, nose, lips, and chin. Luke watched Salm sip on the bourbon and shift her weight this way and that on the bar stool. She liked the way he rolled his glass between his fingertips. Their eyes were trying to establish some kind of trust, to communicate with each other using a language that doesn't require vocabulary and syntax. They started to share the same field of energy. It orbited around them and through them.

Finally, Luke took a deep breath. "You know what?" he asked, breaking the silence.

"What?" She hoped he wasn't going to tell her to leave, to say something like, "I have to go to work," or anything that would transform the warmth mingling around them.

Instead of looking at her face, Luke spoke to the hair that hung around Salm's cheek. "I think I could be crazy about you." Then he looked into her eyes and smiled.

Salm felt her stomach contract. His words knocked the air right out of her. She felt as if she could throw up or maybe she would burst with exaltation. After a split second she simmered down. "*Could* be crazy about me?" she asked, slightly shy, feeling like a teenager learning about the chemistry of crushes and sexual anxiety for the first time.

"OK. Am. Am crazy about you."

She paused to rally the courage to respond. "Yeah," she said. "I'm crazy about you too."

Luke filled their glasses with more bourbon. He lifted his to a toast, and Salm mimicked the gesture. "To the human slices," she said quietly, feeling terrified and happy at the same time.

Their eyes made visual connections that coiled around each other, twisting and entangling tighter and tighter. Without breaking their locked gaze, they gulped the bourbon, and enjoyed the way its heat burned into their throats.

"To the film," Luke toasted.

"And to the bicycle accident," she said.

They clinked glasses again. Luke scooted his bar stool closer to Salm. Then, he moved in to kiss her. He gently took her face into his hands and she felt his long fingers caress her cheeks. It was the kind of kiss that was simply a brushing of his lips across the corner of her mouth. His lips felt dry and cold. Salm, in turn, touched his cheekbones and followed the contours of his face with the tiny nail of her malformed finger. He liked the way the small appendage felt against his late afternoon stubble of beard.

He kissed her again, this time pressing his thumbs across her cheeks, her face glowing from the yellow candle light.

They kissed once more, exploring by touch each other's faces, gently pulling at the flesh. Their mouths were unclean. They tasted good to each other.

Salm felt her nerve endings stretch and come out of hiding. Her physical reaction to his kiss was like feeling snails trail down her back and arms. With every touch, the hair follicles on Luke's body came alive and dug into his skin, all needles and tacks and straight pins, coaxing and pricking. Their lips pressed, their tongues explored. Under the slight pressure of each kiss, their flesh seemed to swell, burst, and decompose. The discomfort was bearable, in its own tormenting way. The only thing that existed for them now was the exquisite sensation of flesh upon flesh. Under the power of cheeks nuzzling cheeks, fears and questions melted and blurred and disappeared. Their flesh fed their flesh and nurtured the need for more. Lips sought lips, and sought necks and eyes and ears.

They pulled each other off of their barstools while slowly, slowly pulling off the protection of socks, shirts, and pants. They took time to look at each other and smile innocent, inviting smiles.

Salm kissed his shoulders and collarbone, taking in his scent. He caressed her breasts and rubbed his lips across her stiff nipples. They eased in slow motion toward the bed, still not sure of who was following whom, but very sure of each other's dance. No one was in a hurry.

The sink behind the bar kept dripping.

# IX

Come morning, the slight hum of the public address system nudged Salm from a deep sleep. She was spread across the bed, lying on her stomach, trying to remember if she had only dreamed of dramatic, extravagant sex and lots of bourbon or if something really happened.

Luke stood on the stage and pressed his lips against the microphone. "Testing one-two. Testing one-two." He waited for Salm to untangle herself from the sheets. And while he waited, his eyes followed the curved lines of the red vinyl booth across the room. They were like the booths at Caesar's Palace. He had been there once. Years ago, his friend George won a trip to Las Vegas, and Luke went with him. They didn't do much. They went to the lounge shows that featured bare breasts and bad comedians, but the rest of the time they simply roamed in and around the casinos, periodically taken in by the one-armed bandits, although neither of them really enjoyed gambling. Gambling produced hope and expectations. At that time in their lives, they had little appreciation of those abstracts.

Luke leaned into the microphone again. "Testing one-two. Testing."

Salm's bare feet stuck out from under the sheets, and she flexed the toes on her right foot to let him know that she was gaining momentum.

He leaned over to the amplifier and turned up the volume. "Testing one-two. Testing." Salm's face hung over the bed. The hum of the public address system grew louder.

Luke began to growl, a low, quiet growl, like an angry cat. Then he stopped. Salm still didn't move. So he growled louder and louder, raising the pitch until his growl turned into the yelp of a lonely coyote.

Salm, feeling uncertain and self-conscious, couldn't make herself turn over and look at him. Luke stood motionless on the stage, waiting for a response.

He pushed his lips up against the microphone and formed an "O" with his mouth. He breathed deeply, sending smooth, rhythmic pulses of monkey sounds through the speakers. He grunted, quietly at first. Then the grunts became more self-assured and animated until he was wailing the best imitation of jungle primates that he could, bellowing and whooping as he scratched his head, pounded his chest, and snorted hot breath.

Finally, Salm rolled over. Self-consciousness be damned. This, she had to see.

Luke was naked, his limp penis flailing from side to side, as he lurched around the stage. He scratched his armpits and gasped out the sounds of gorilla mating rituals, his performance gaining more energy now that Salm had stretched out on her side to watch him.

She laughed and held out her arms toward him. He responded to the gesture, and with simian swings of his arms and legs, he gorilla-walked to the bed and landed next to her on his square, strong knees.

Salm dismissed the misty feeling in her head, and shot up on her haunches, joining Luke nose to nose. She picked at his scalp and sniffed his hair, then sucked on a strand of it. He sniffed her back, grooming her neck and ears. But suddenly, the game was over.

"I've got to go," Luke said. "I've got to go for a walk."

"Right now?"

"Yeah. Right now. I've been up for a couple of hours, and well, yeah, I just have to get outside." He sat on the edge of the bed and sucked on her miniature finger. He kissed her again and her response was limp.

"Stick around," he said. "I won't be gone long."

"Can't."

A voice blasted in through the speakers on the stage. "Good morning, Luke, my friend!"

Luke threw himself back on the bed.

"Where's that voice coming from?" Salm sat up in bed and covered her chest. Her eyes darted around the room.

"Across the street. It's Mitch." Luke didn't think any other explanation was in order.

The voice boomed through the speakers again. "I bet you're feeling good this fine morning."

"Who's Mitch?" Salm felt exposed and threatened by the presence of the voice.

"He lives across the street. He's this old guy who lives across the street—shit, since I was a baby."

"Well, that explains it."

Luke sighed. He didn't like sarcasm. "It's just that he knows I'm probably feeling great—with you here and everything."

"How does he know I'm here?" Salm pulled the sheet around her. She surveyed the room again for hidden video cameras.

"He watches me."

"Watches you?" Salm clasped the sheet tighter.

"He can't see inside. Don't worry." Luke pulled the sheet from Salm so that he could see her breasts. "He just watches everybody's comings and goings on the street. It gives him something to do. He must have seen you come in yesterday . . . and assumed you never left."

Salm took her eyes off the speakers and glanced at Luke. "You're always that successful with women?" Luke didn't answer, so Salm went back to the subject of Mitch. "But where's his voice coming from?"

"His ham radio."

"Really? How?"

"He operates on the same frequency as my p.a. system. That's why I leave it on all the time."

"And he can butt in just like that?"

"Yeah."

"Can he hear us?"

"Not at all."

Luke turned to her, dragging his finger across the softness of her inner thigh. "It's good contact, for both of us. He's kind of reclusive. If he needs something, I'm just a radio wave away."

Luke stroked Salm's arm as they lay still and listened to Mitch's breath come through the speakers. It was heavy, low breathing. Salm realized that all three of them were inhaling and exhaling to the same beat.

Mitch interrupted again, this time quietly. "Yes, miss, you ought to know that Luke is a good man." Salm looked from the speakers to Luke, who was now absent-mindedly pulling at his pubic hairs, still smiling.

"Did you coach him on that?" she asked.

"Come for a walk with me," Luke said. He got up to grab the basketball that rested against the stage.

"Can't. I have to leave." Even though she was the one turning down an invitation, Salm felt a bit rejected and insufficient.

Luke put the basketball on the floor. "Have to leave or want to leave?" He disappeared into the bathroom.

"Have to," she said, hoping Luke heard. She flopped back in the bed and buried her head in a pillow, cocooning herself into the sheets. She felt that she did have to leave. And she was afraid Luke wouldn't ask to see her again.

He came back into the bar dressed in jeans and a sweatshirt. He desperately needed to get outside. The air seemed to be getting thin. His body was restless and anxious.

But right before he left, he picked up the basketball he left near the stage, and from across the room, he looked at Salm, who was now a big lump wound into his sheets. His mouth gulped a deep breath. "Don't worry about it," he said. "I'm still crazy about you."

He stood there and felt stupid, imagining that his words were wrong. Salm couldn't believe how right they were. Motionless, she stayed under cover, frozen with glee. She listened to Luke open the front door and let in the sounds of traffic. The crunch of the metal burglar gate closed behind him, and she heard his dribbling basketball echo down Damen Avenue.

Salm wished that she had said something to him, but the words got stuck. She was afraid to acknowledge his sentence and afraid to make her own. She had learned long ago that people said things they didn't mean to say, or said what they meant to say and then decided later they didn't mean what they said at all.

Luke and his basketball bounced steadily and evenly down the street. He knew he would go where his legs would take him. He tried not to think about Salm. He chose to forget that he had just told a woman that he was crazy about her for right now. Right now, he felt like running down to "The Bee Hive" for some scrambled eggs.

# X

Humming a very happy tune indeed, Salm got up and went to the front door to lock it, and as she flipped the deadbolt into place, Mitch's voice came through the public address system again.

"Yes, ma'am, he's a fine one, that Luke."

Salm stood still, waiting for more, but all she heard was Mitch's slow, steady breath. She moved to the stage and leaned into the microphone. "Thanks for the information," she said. "Thanks. Thanks a lot." She wanted to sound nice and to make a good impression, even though she knew Mitch couldn't hear her.

She grabbed her bag, went to the door marked "Ladies," and proceeded to go through a makeshift morning ritual that included her pulling at the dark circles under her eyes and mumbling something to herself about getting old. She shivered as she sat down on the cold toilet seat, and she buried her head in her hands, not knowing if she should laugh or if she should cry. She decided on neither and got up to dunk her head under the ice cold water that sputtered from the rusty faucet.

There wasn't any toilet paper or soap in this room. Salm interpreted that to mean Luke probably didn't have women around very often. Or else, it was possible, she thought, that he had women around all of the time, but he just didn't bother keeping up with the amenities in the "Ladies Room" of an old bar. Why would he? She was annoyed with her need to analyze and second guess, angry with herself because she was thinking about pasts and futures, and she just met the man.

She wandered into the Men's Room and found Luke's mangled toothbrush, its bristles bent and curved. With it, she scrubbed her teeth until she eliminated the stale taste of bourbon in her mouth. The bathroom mirror was dotted with white specks and smudges and dribbles. She widely smiled at her reflection and imagined what her Aunt Elaine would have said: "Don't ever end up in an awkward, I've-overstayed-my-welcome situation, Salm. A lady always knows when to leave. Remember that. When you know when to say goodbye, you'll have a better chance at another 'hello.'"

She knew Aunt Elaine was right, but she wanted a little more time.

She went back behind the bar, remembering seeing a coffee maker there last night. She was surprised and very pleased that Luke had brewed a fresh pot. After choosing a ceramic mug from under the bar, she looked inside of it and blew out the dust. Her eyes followed the gray design of cracks on the mug. She imagined that Luke's eyes could do that to the cup. One of his simple stares, so hot and so cold at the same time, could make the cup slowly start to fracture, one crack leading to another crack, and then to another. He could do the same to her. She could tell.

After she poured herself a cup of strong coffee, she scooted into one of the booths, the one whose table was filled with mannequin arms. Each plastic limb had a rusted screw sticking out from the upper arm stub. Salm stroked the arms and examined the chipped red polish on the perfectly shaped fingers. While she sipped her coffee, she aimlessly measured the shape of her malformed finger against those of the mannequins.

She then made her way into the back of the bar and found an industrial-sized kitchen, a makeshift shower, and lots of storage space. She couldn't help but make a cursory inspection of Luke's belongings, and was especially intrigued by the presence of an artificial leg hanging from a giant hook on the wall. The leg seemed to be watching her. "Too weird," she said, hesitantly touching it. The fact that Luke owned female mannequins and had removed their arms did not register points in his favor, but his owning a plastic leg did. Salm decided to think about why that was so later.

In the shower, she let the hot water pound onto her back and shoulders and top of her head while she sang, "Never Never Land." It was one of her favorites when she was feeling sappy and contented, beleaguered and confused. But she had to go, she had work to do. Wendy was coming over today. She wanted Salm to make something for her mother for Mother's Day.

Rummaging through a drawer behind the bar, Salm found a self-adhesive note pad and slapped a message onto the breast of one of the armless mannequins. She wrote: 2336 West Haydon, 2nd floor (use the back door). She didn't want to leave her number. She would rather hope for Luke's company than for a phone call. She wanted to touch him again. His voice alone wouldn't be enough.

# XI

Luke sat at the counter of "The Bee." At some of his favorite diners, he preferred booths or tables. But at this one, the counter was best. It was one of those square-shaped, center-of-the-room counters. Any seat was a good one for watching the waitresses, the customers, the tubs of dirty dishes, the cigarette butts on the floor. Luke's eyes focused on some boxes of saltines stacked near the kitchen. He thought of Salm again and tried to get the smirk off his face. He didn't want anyone to suspect that he had just left a woman alone in his place—one, no less, he had just told, "I'm crazy about you."

He read the morning paper. Or, rather he tried to read it. The words swam on the page as if they were in a hurry to get somewhere and they needed to run from his gaze. Luke hated it when a woman scrambled his concentration. It took him a long time to make sense out of the comics.

After he devoured two eggs over medium, well done bacon, and slightly burnt toast, he slurped down another cup of coffee while skimming the editorial pages in the newspaper. Satisfied, he stretched. He wanted to play basketball.

Luke didn't follow the statistics and commentary of professional sports, basketball or any other kind. He didn't care about those things. He only loved to play. For years now, from the first warm day of the year through the crispness of fall, he had played in the mornings at Clemente High School with his friend George, but so far this spring, George hadn't shown up.

George's wife had recently left him. He hadn't said much about it to Luke except, "I need time to get over the shock of it, that's all." Luke said he would let him. So things went on. Luke played basketball assuming that one day George would join him again.

Luke had never been married, not even close. He had only slipped here and there (or was led) into relationships that were sometimes satisfactory, sometimes not. Mostly, he tried to avoid any suffering that would result from a personal attachment (or detachment), but he had not been completely successful. He understood the basic sense of heartache and had, at one time or another, felt abandoned and vulnerable, but he also knew the experience of complete recovery. He told George, "Things will work out for the best, whatever that may be."

As Luke jogged across the school ground, he could feel upon him the stares of students who were locked up for the last weeks of school. He didn't mind that his neighbor Mitch watched him, perched on the second floor across the street, but the presence of the students' eyes bothered him. He would be glad when summer vacation came, and the students would be gone. He liked the basketball court best in the summer, just as the sun rose. The hushed silence, the eerie light of dawn, and the thud of the basketball—those were the things that made perfect mornings. For now, he would ignore the vague faces that gazed out at him from the school building.

Luke was a good basketball player, and he felt awkward about being so good. There was something very bold and big about playing well. His legs and arms worked under their own power and instincts. They stretched, turned, twisted, and twirled with liquid speed. And while his body worked, the steady thud of the ball put him into an almost meditative state. He would feel charged and centered, at the same time, conscious and unconscious. Sometimes, he found answers to the mundane (and the sublime) questions in his life in the spin of the ball, the reverberation of the backboard, and in the breaths of hot air that escaped from his lungs.

This morning, if George were around, Luke might have told him about Salm. No, not might have. He surely would have. In all of their years of friendship—from adolescence until now in their thirty-seventh year—they were always in synch with where they were in their lives. The geek years. The Playboy magazine years. The pot-smoking years. The angst-ridden art school years. The still angst-ridden adult years. But then, just last summer, George had flung himself boldly out of his and Luke's shared orbit forever. He had simply decreed, "Ever since I was a kid, I knew that I wanted to be a dad, so that's what I'm going to do. Part of who I am is a dad, you know?"

Luke stumbled through his answer, "No, not, not really." He looked at George as if he suddenly were a man he never knew.

"I know we've never talked about it. But it was a matter of time, that's all, a matter of me accepting being a man, being responsible," George continued. Luke remained dumbfounded. It was a conversation he never would have imagined.

And then George asked, "You know what else?"

"No. I can't imagine. What else?"

"I'm going to marry Gail. We're going the whole ten yards."

Luke looked at the ceiling and then at the floor. He wondered how someone could become so unfamiliar in only seconds. "Wow" was all he said.

"Congratulations?" George asked.

"Yeah. Sure. Congratulations."

"It's OK with you, isn't it, that me and Gail . . ."

Luke shrugged. "No problem. Really. Great."

And that was that.

Gail was one of Luke's former lovers. After he and Gail stopped seeing each other, she had started "hanging out" with George, and hanging out quickly turned into an intense, monogamous relationship—something that George had previously avoided. Luke thought that maybe Gail was trying to punish him somehow, trying to make him want her and miss her, but Luke never said anything to George about it. There was no reason. George seemed happier than he had ever been. Gail appeared ecstatic. Maybe they really were in love. Luke didn't think it would last, however. George had always been committed to staying unattached, and Luke knew Gail wanted a child. In fact, it was one of the reasons Luke stopped seeing her.

Luke could recall her late night pleadings with him. "All I want is a father for the baby," she would confess, sometimes a little weepy. "I want you to be the father. Please. I love you." Luke couldn't accept the offered role. He cared about Gail very much but certainly wasn't ready to make a commitment to a child, let alone to Gail. She would go on, "It doesn't matter. I'll raise it alone. I'm not asking anything of you." Luke would just shake his head. No. For him, that wasn't the way it was going to work.

"Then I'll find someone else who will love me."

"OK," Luke had told her.

In only months, Gail and George were planning a very small wedding, with some family, a few friends, and an unconventional ceremony in the Indiana Dunes. A "pagan celebration of our love" is what Gail called it. Luke would often find himself looking at the two of them as if they had been abducted, possessed, and reprogrammed. But then he would look at them again, and he would see that they were truly happy. Fairy tale happy.

The night before the wedding, George and Luke got drunk together. "All this love and marriage crap, you know," George said, "I like it. I used to be so damn sure that nobody, absolutely nobody, could satisfy somebody else's wants and needs. I mean, what do you get when you try to do that?"

"Grief and aggravation?" Luke answered.

"Usually that's the case. You're right. But this is different with Gail, you know? She's got 'I wants' and 'I needs' and they fucking match my wants and needs. They fucking match, Luke. For the first time, it's like I'm in a real partnership. A unit. And I'm not scared. I'm not fucking scared of it."

"Like part of you isn't dying?"

George laughed. "Yeah. Like part of me isn't dying."

"Even though it has . . ."

George paused and thought. "Yeah. You're right. Part of me *has* died. No, wait. It hasn't died; evolved, rather. But that's what happens. That's life. Personal evolution." He looked earnestly at his friend. "And I am so happy that this is the way my life is going." Luke nodded and George went on. "Gail and me . . . we're a living cliché, man. We've been doing the domestic shit together, creating this couple persona, and there's gonna be a whole new life from it. We're perpetuating the species. We're fucking affirming life, for Christ's sake."

Luke, bleary eyed, listened politely. "Affirming life?" he thought. "Where is he getting this stuff?" Nonetheless, Luke was pleased to see that George's immersion into the traditions of marriage and fatherhood brought him such bliss. A person can tire of relentless cynicism. Luke waved his beer bottle over George's head in a blessing. "Go in peace, my friend. Be fruitful and multiply."

George laughed. "It's worth giving in to it, man. It's really gonna be worth it. " He waved his own beer bottle over Luke's head. "May ye seek and find yours." Then they went and played pinball.

Luke spun the basketball on his index finger. Out of the corner of his eye, he saw a student walking across the school grounds. He was probably cutting World History. That's what Luke would have cut on a day like today. World History. The student's t-shirt said "Just Say No," and Luke had a passing thought that sometimes it wasn't that easy, or maybe it wasn't that smart to say no. He imagined Salm dancing around his bar in a gauzy toga, drinking coffee, looking through his belongings. But he quickly shook the fantasy from his mind. No. It was easy to say no. It always had been, for both him and George. And the one time George didn't say no, looked what happened.

When Gail left George, she was more than four months pregnant with his child. George still didn't know where she had gone. She hadn't made contact with him. But she periodically called Luke, sometimes sobbing, sometimes perfunctory. Luke would say, "You've got to talk to him, Gail." She would say things back to Luke like "Fuck" or "Christ" or "You don't understand." And always, "I'm so very scared of what's happening to me."

Luke damned himself for having told Salm that he was crazy about her. He hoped she didn't take him too seriously.

He got up to shoot a thirty footer. The basketball hit the backboard and fell through the hoop. He high-fived an imaginary vision of George and took off toward home. He hoped Salm would be gone. He wondered if she had left her number. Then again, he hoped she had not.

# XII

George arrived at the Clemente basketball courts minutes after Luke had left. He wasn't making an effort to keep track of time. If he saw Luke, he saw him. If he didn't, that was OK too.

His fellow instructors at the Art Institute were busy grading final projects and planning their summer adventures to Europe, South America, and Asia, to paint and film other worlds and other lives. They didn't notice that George was operating on a kind of automatic pilot since Gail left him. He didn't say hello or good-bye to anyone, and no one said hello or good-bye to him either.

George's parents knew Gail was gone, but they didn't press him for information when they called on Sunday nights. He had long ago trained his mother not to nag or to be too involved in his personal life. "She'll be back, George," is all his mother would say. "She needs you."

And Gail's family? Her parents were dead, and she had one sister, Elise. When Gail left, George assumed she had found refuge at her sister's house, and he made an unexpected visit to her front door. Elise was calm. She talked to George through the screen. "Gail's not here, George. But she's OK."

"Has she called you?"

"No."

"Then how do you know she's OK?"

"Gail's always OK. You're just going to have to wait." She smiled at George as if she understood how alone and confused he felt.

"What could I have done to make her leave?" he asked, his voice sounding frail and thin.

"You didn't do anything, George. Believe that. She's just afraid."

"Of me?"

Elise was still smiling. "No, not at you. Afraid of what's happening. You know, you two haven't been together all that long." Elise opened the door and sat down on the front steps. As soon as George sat next to her, she sighed. "How do I explain? Gail's always been a 'bolter.'"

George looked blankly at her.

"You know. She bolts."

"No. I don't know."

"When Gail's not sure of what's happening to her, when she's afraid, when, I don't know, when the physical stuff over powers everything, she's been known to run away. I was actually surprised that she didn't run away before your wedding."

"That would have been stupid."

"I'm not saying if it would be stupid or not. But Gail was so happy. She was getting everything she wanted, and she was so damn happy she glowed. Isn't there some old saying like, 'Watch out. You might get what you ask for'? She had become a different person with you. And that's just about the time Gail runs from something, when she becomes different, when she changes." Elise chuckled a little. "I remember when we were girls and she got her first period, she ran away to one of our cousins in Wisconsin. My aunt couldn't get her to come home for two weeks."

George smiled.

"Sometimes it's easy moving into new roles, but sometimes those big changes can scare the living be-Jesus out of you, George. With me and Tom, for example. We had been involved all through high school, then college. By the time we got married, well, it was so natural. Moving into parenthood was easy for us. But with you and Gail, it's different, I suppose."

George looked at her. "Why should we be different?"

"Oh, I don't know. You two knew so clearly and so intuitively what you wanted, and you were able to make it happen with each other. And it was so fast. Who knows? You might start to wonder, to second guess yourself. Did I make this happen because I want it, or is some other internal power calling the shots? Am I doing what I'm supposed to be doing? Is this my life? Is this really what I want with my life? Those kinds of questions, you know?" Elise touched George on the shoulder. "But everything will be fine, George. Really."

He looked at her as if he didn't believe her.

"Stay in touch," she said. "If you hear anything. Or if I hear anything . . ."

And George hadn't spoken to Elise since then. He didn't know what to believe or to think. He only mourned, replaying in his mind, over and over, every minute, every day that he and Gail shared together, trying to find a clue.

The simple note had been taped to the bathroom mirror: "I have to leave. I can't explain it, but I do love you and our baby." She hadn't signed her name.

He remembered taking the note off the mirror and holding it, staring at it, curling the edges of the paper under his fingertips, and feeling an awful power lifting off the top of his head, pouring hot lava into his blood stream and leaving something angry and vile surging and pressing through his veins. Now, it still simmered inside of him.

How could he ever understand her betrayal? He had purposely been a solitary person most of his time on earth, and through her, he had changed that position, wholeheartedly embracing the traditions of the human race and entering its unfamiliar universe. They had begun a life together, then created a life together. He had welcomed the bonds of marriage and parenthood only to have Gail cruelly cut them away.

Summer would finally come and George wouldn't do much during his days. He would hang around their apartment, often spending time leafing through Gail's things. She had taken very little with her. Or he would wander his neighborhood, stopping at his two favorite places– the bench down the street at the Damen bus stop and Mike's, a little tavern. Sitting (or lying) on the bus stop bench, he would watch people wait for the bus, board the bus, get off the bus. At Mike's, he would sit for hours, watching the beer in his glass or the television suspended from the ceiling.

Most of the time, he would think about the questions he wanted to ask his wife. He didn't know if she was miserable in second grade as he had been, or if she had cried at the end of "Close Encounters of the Third Kind" the way he always did, if she had liked Ernie Kovacs, his own idol. They had earnestly wanted a baby and they got one. Didn't she realize how lucky they were? How could she have walked away?

# XIII

Salm, Wendy, and Claire were right to laugh at Sylvia that morning outside of the diner. Even though she continually insisted she was going to end her relationship with Armando, her friends always knew it was just talk. That afternoon, when Sylvia went home (where she and Armando had lived together for more than a year and where he had yet to contribute to the rent), he didn't turn off the television, but he did open his fly and say, "Suck it." As soon as she sank to her knees, she wiped out any thoughts of how she was wasting her life, any thoughts of tallying up how much money he owed her and asking him to pack his bags. It was easier to deny her humiliation.

Later that night, she and Armando smoked a joint and opened a bottle of good red wine. They started to watch a rented movie but it didn't keep their interest. Instead, Armando led Sylvia to bed where he sweetly made love to her. Afterwards, he fell asleep and she watched him with tenderness and, at the same time, with hostility. How she wished she could separate herself from him. She had come to the realization, painfully, that she no longer loved him, if she ever did. Yet she wanted to be attached to someone. She wanted constancy. She loathed the idea of starting a search for man who may or may not be any better than Armando. He was kind, or rather, could be kind. He cared for her as much as she cared for him. She hated herself for it, but she knew she was completely submerged in a classic case of "settling" until something better came along, that is, if she ever chose to look for something better.

She quietly pulled herself out of bed and headed to the living room. There was still some wine left. She sat quietly, feeling empty and unconnected, the way she felt when she had the flu.

She awakened just before dawn. After she made herself some coffee, she curled back up on the couch with her all-time favorite book—a biography of St. John of the Cross. She especially liked the chapter that described his death scene. She read and re-read it.

When St. John died, his body was covered with cancerous sores that oozed puss and disease. The people who knew of his death, anticipating his sainthood, swarmed into the cubicle where he lay. They all wanted to get a piece of him, an important relic to adore. The mourners ripped at his flesh, and it was recorded that some of them actually sucked on the lesions. They tore at his hair and wrenched out his fingernails. One exceptionally zealous lamenter gnawed off St. John's big toe. Sylvia loved that part.

After reading awhile, she crawled back into bed with Armando, careful not to touch him. She just needed to lie still and to rest her eyes. She feigned sleep when he awoke. He often wanted to make love in the morning, and she knew she would be unable to bear his touch. She listened to him in the kitchen, heard him in the shower, then finally close the front door. She was glad to be alone and quickly got up.

Sylvia spent the rest of the morning sitting at her kitchen window, watching the occasional car pass down her quiet residential street. She drank more coffee, flipped through the newspaper, and chewed her fingernails. She tried to call Salm a few times, but there was no answer.

Sylvia liked sitting at her kitchen window. It gave her a good view of her whole neighborhood—the houses, the high school, and the park. She watched people come and go from blocks away. The distance made them faceless, moving things, but she knew their patterns. She knew who took what bus when, who got home at what time, who mowed their lawn, who bought new furniture. She knew who played basketball in the morning.

Today she watched the tall man with the long hair. He was later than usual today, and he didn't play for too long, probably because he was alone again. She wondered what had happened to his friend. They used to play together every day.

Sylvia's hobby was worrying about all the solitary people she saw. Fretting about them was in her blood. She was a professional volunteer.

On Tuesdays, she cooked for the homeless at a South Side soup kitchen. On Wednesdays, she read to the blind and taught phonics to the illiterate at the library. Every other Saturday, she would get high at home and then go to the community center to counsel teenagers with drug abuse problems. But her favorite volunteer activity was for the humane society—taking puppies to Children's Memorial Hospital to coerce parents with sick children to adopt a pet.

After college, Sylvia got a job as a counselor at Catholic Charities, and a few evenings a week, she volunteered at a nursing home. There, she had taken a special interest in one old man who had had a stroke. His name was Walter. Sylvia read to him, took him to physical therapy and applauded when he was finally able to lift a spoon to his lips. She spent weeks trying to locate even the most remote family members, but to no avail. Over the weeks, then months, they became each other's family. (Sylvia had long been estranged from her own.) She and Walter grew to love each other very much and depended upon each other for comfort and company. They spent Christmas Days together. Finally, he died one night while Sylvia held his hand. He left her his savings, stock portfolio, insurance, and more.

Sylvia had been thrilled with her newfound wealth, not because of what she could buy or where she could go, but because now she could give money as well as her time to those who needed it. She lived frugally and gave generously.

She met Armando while she was delivering meals to AIDS patients. A local diner voluntarily prepared the food, and Sylvia would load up her car with covered dishes. For a special touch, before making the deliveries, she would go down to the Randolph Street flower market to buy babies' breath and carnations or asters for simple little bud vases. She made sure everyone would get flowers at least once a week. Armando worked at the flower market. His brother had died of AIDS. They were immediately connected.

She could recall how she would count the days between her trips for flowers, how disappointed she would be if Armando wasn't there when she arrived. His smile had lit a spark inside of her and that one spark exploded into a hot blue saintly glow that she thought would shine and shine forever. In a few months, he moved in with her, and the next day, the glow slowly started to dim.

While Sylvia sat and looked out the window, she bit too hard on a piece of flesh around her index finger and it bled. She really didn't want to be alone. She poured herself more coffee and dialed Salm's number again.

# XIV

Salm picked up the phone on the first ring. "Yeah, sure, Sylvia," she said. "Just Wendy and the baby and Michael. Come on over."

Salm went back to her company. "Sylvia's on her way."

"Is she all mopey about Armando?"

"What else?"

Wendy shook her head, not looking forward to hearing more about the depressing saga of Sylvia's disappointing relationship. Michael, Salm's upstairs neighbor, sipped on wine from an old shrimp cocktail glass. He said, "How long is she going to stay with that guy?"

"It's almost a tragedy."

"No, my life is almost a tragedy."

"No, your life *is* a tragedy."

Wendy laughed and readjusted Matthew, her nine-month old son, on her lap. He chewed on his balled up fist and drool ran from his mouth in long, uneven strands.

A plastic squirt bottle, a leftover supply from one of Salm's hair color changes, was now used as a paint applicator. Salm shook it and put a finishing splat of red on a scarf pinned to her print table. She looked at Wendy. "I hope you appreciate that I passed up a perfectly fine invitation to play basketball for you."

"Hey, you had a choice."

"Mother's Day. Jesus. Why did I tell you I would do something for your mother for Mother's Day? I'm not even sending my own mother anything."

"My mother likes your stuff."

"It won't please her anyway." Salm hated doing artwork for friends. She was always afraid of disappointing them.

"You know the reason you can't please your mothers is that you always anticipate their rejection," Michael piped in. He sat on the floor, his head thrown back against the wall. "Expect some positive feedback once in awhile."

Wendy and Salm looked at each other with raised eyebrows. "It's a mother-daughter thing, Michael. You can't please them. Ever." Wendy shifted Matthew to her other thigh. She wished she could put him down and let him crawl, but Salm's entire living room was taken up by her massive print table, and the floor was littered with hundreds of bottles and cans and jars of paint. Rags, spatulas, sponges, and brushes were stacked everywhere.

Salm looked at the baby and saw parts of Wendy's face emerge from his. But there was another image there, the image of the father. All of Wendy's friends enjoyed wondering about the man who donated his sperm to make this little baby he would never see. When they walked down the street together, Salm and Claire and the others would often play a game to try to identify a stranger as the possible father, a man who would beat off in a test tube for posterity.

Wendy never wondered about the father at all. The baby belonged only to her.

Salm pulled the t-pins out of the scarf and lifted the stretch of fabric straight off the table. She carried it down the long hall that led to her kitchen where clotheslines sagged this way and that way from wall to wall. Her hand-painted scarves blew slightly from the breeze that filtered through her screen door. She tested a white scarf doused with trickles of blood red paint to see if it was dry. She had to have these scarves delivered tomorrow. Tonight, she would go to the laundromat to heat set them. Besides her medical illustration work, Salm had created a little sideline business in fabric design—with most of the patterns and motifs based on the shapes and constructs of viruses, bacteria, and diseased blood cells (and nobody seemed to notice or mind the connection).

Salm looked at the bolts of fabric, the gauzes, and silks that were stacked on her floor-to-ceiling pantry shelves. She walked back into the living room carrying a shrink-wrapped white sheet.

"Take Matthew's clothes off," she said as she began tacking the sheet to the print table.

"What for?"

"I've been inspired. Let's let Matthew paint a mural for his grandma. I can think of no better Mother's Day present than a grandson-made work of art."

"Are you kidding?"

"No, hand him over here. I'll soak his little piggies and his teenie weenie fingies and let him go for it." Salm grabbed at the baby's feet and tickled him. "Won't that be fun, little guy?" Then she poured bright yellow paint into a rolling pan.

"He'll eat the paint, Salm. You can't let a baby roll in paint."

"It's okay if he eats this stuff. He can drink a gallon and it won't hurt him."

Wendy clutched her child.

"Jesus Christ, Wendy." Michael spoke to the ceiling and rolled his eyes at Salm.

Salm grabbed Matthew from his mother. "Yeah, Jesus Christ, Wendy. It'll be fine." Salm tickled Matt's toes again and dipped them into the yellow paint. He squealed from the cold wetness. Once his feet were soaked, Salm held him by his fingertips and walked him across the crisp white sheet. Both the mother and the son giggled while Salm wrested the remainder of his clothes from him and squirted his rear with robin's egg blue.

"You're asking for trouble taking off his diaper," Wendy said.

"It'll wash out if he pees," Salm replied. Salm sponged reds and oranges and greens on Matt's soft skin and rolled him around on the fabric.

Wendy sat there and shook her head, watching Salm and Matthew laughing and playing. Wendy thought it sad that Salm, who was being so wonderful with Matt, would never have her own children. She looked at Michael and thought the same for him.

Michael understood the expression on Wendy's face. "Oh, please, Wendy," he said. "Just because Salm is having fun with Matthew doesn't mean she wants one of her very own."

Salm smiled at Michael in appreciation. He poured himself more wine and tossed his hair away from his face. "So let me tell you what happened next," he said.

The women exchanged somewhat exasperated glances. Michael had been taking a long time getting his story out.

"Where were you?" Wendy asked.

"On the couch. I was lounging on the couch smoking a cigarette."

Salm kept playing with Matt while she talked to Wendy and Michael. "What did you have on? Your kimono or smoking jacket?"

"Smoking jacket, of course. I was being very gothic." Michael smiled, pleased with himself, and tossed his hair again. "So you should have seen my living room. I had all the lights turned off, and I don't even know, maybe twenty, thirty candles burning."

"Incense?"

"The 'Do As I Say' kind from the voodoo museum."

"And then?"

"Well, Richard was lying on the floor, staring up at the ceiling, looking completely preoccupied. Smug. You know?"

Neither woman had met Richard, but had heard about him quite extensively in the last few weeks. He was an actor. He used a cigarette holder and wore a beret over his gleaming, thick, and wavy black hair. He had one blue eye and one brown one. Michael was dazzled by him and followed him home from a bookstore. Sleeping with him had become Michael's obsession.

For a minute, they all watched Matthew rub his face into the globs of paint on the sheet. Wendy was appalled, but decided to trust Salm about the paint being non-toxic.

"So what happened?"

"Well, I was trying to be casual, even though I was ready to piss all over myself I was so nervous. I mean, why should I be nervous? Who knows? But you should have seen this incredible pose I struck—kind of

Julie London-ish. It was great. And then Richard tells me I can touch his hair if I want. Do you believe him?"

Salm and Wendy wailed simultaneously: "He gave you permission to touch his hair?"

"Uh-huh. Isn't that insane? But I'm ready for the big seduction, so I don't care. Anyway, then I get up to change the music and I put on that really grand, sweeping Puccini piece, *Turandot*, however you say it, and it blares through the speakers and I'm ready for the big scene now, especially because Richard gets up and stands in front of me as I'm walking back from the stereo. I'm about ready to bust, of course. "

"Then what?" Wendy leaned over, anxious to hear the rest.

"So then," Michael said, laughing, "Richard kisses me on the cheek really sweetly and says he has to leave!"

"What!?"

"Yeah. Do you believe that? Here I am ready for sex with the man of my dreams and he decides it's time to leave. Just fucking time to leave!"

"Just like that."

"Just like that. Gotta go. Bye-bye. See ya in church."

"What did you say?"

"I was in shock. I couldn't say anything. I just stood there with my mouth open and watched him go toward the door. He was walking slowly and then he turned and he looked at me as if I was the total scum of the earth, like some putrescence, some evil, as if I did anything to deserve that, and he says—'Jesus, Michael, what do you think this is, with this music and candles and all this shit. What do you think this is? A fucking movie? It's just sex, man.' And he walked out the door, the fuck."

"Oh, man," Wendy sympathized.

Salm nodded in sympathy too. "What a fuck is right. 'It's just sex, man'?"

"Yeah, how about that? Just sex. It's like the driving force of the entire fucking universe, and he says 'It's just sex, man.'"

"And to add insult to injury, he doesn't even think you're worthy."

"Fuck you."

Salm guarded Matthew to make sure he wouldn't fall off the table, and reached for her wine. She heard a knock at her back door. "It's open. We're in front, Syl!" she yelled. Salm picked up Matthew and handed the baby over to Wendy, who held her son at arm's length, trying to keep herself free of paint.

Salm headed toward the kitchen. But it wasn't Sylvia at the back door. It was Luke. He had already come in and was swimming through the damp scarves crisscrossing the clotheslines stretched across the kitchen. Salm felt the wine hit her. A film of sweat rose around her scalp. She gulped for air.

"Hi," she said. He nodded at her. Their eyes exchanged affectionate little messages in secret code.

"Hi. Who's Syl?" he said, wiping a strand of hair away from Salm's face.

"Not you." Salm turned and Luke followed her down the hall.

Wendy's and Michael's eyes noticeably widened when Luke followed Salm into the living room. Luke nodded at them. For a moment, Salm's brain froze. She forgot his name. Wendy recognized terror in Salm's eyes and smiled. "Hi. I'm Wendy."

"Michael." Michael and Luke shook hands.

"Luke."

Luke glanced at the empty bottle of wine on the floor next to Michael. "Where are your manners, Salm? Got anything else to drink?" Michael asked.

"Oh, yeah, sorry," she said. "Do you want something?"

Michael started to get up to help out.

"Oh, no, that's OK," Luke said, touching Michael's shoulder. "I'll get it."

Luke left the room to survey Salm's refrigerator. While he did, Salm frantically gestured and mouthed "That's him, that's him" to her friends. Wendy and Michael made distorted, absurd faces, mocking Salm's pantomime. Wendy mouthed, "He's darling." "Darling," mimicked Michael.

Luke stood in front of the open refrigerator feeling out of place and thinking he ought not to have come. He didn't like the silence in the other room. Why weren't they talking? But he grabbed a beer and strolled back into the living room anyway.

"Hi, again," he said, lifting his bottle in a toast.

"Hi, again," Wendy and Michael responded in unison. They tried to look casual, as if they weren't guilty of having some private knowledge of Luke's sexual prowess. Salm had provided them a detailed version of her night with Luke just before Michael had started his own tale.

"That boy needs a good dunk in the bathtub," Luke said, pointing his beer in the direction of Matthew.

"He sure does. This is Matt," Wendy said, repositioning the baby and carrying him down to the bathroom. "What a mess, huh?"

Matthew reached out with his yellow paint covered hand, and Luke reached back. "Hey, little guy." Matthew giggled. Luke's fingers were coated with wet yellow paint now too.

Michael struggled up from his position against the wall. "Let me help," he said, as he followed Wendy down the hall, giving Salm a quick wink as he passed by.

Luke perched on top of one of the stools surrounding Salm's print table. "I sure must've interrupted something. Everybody seems so—uncomfortable."

"I'm sorry. We were . . . I was just so startled by your walking in and I don't know, I didn't know what to say."

"C'mere," he said.

Salm walked over to him, shy and bashful.

"Don't you have a phone?" he asked.

"Yeah, I have a phone."

"Why didn't you leave your number?"

"I figured you wouldn't call."

He smirked. "Did you think I'd come over?"

"Not really."

"Neither did I."

"But I did want to see you."

"Then look at me." Luke smeared yellow paint down Salm's nose, lips, chin, and neck. Then he gently kissed her. When they pulled apart and saw each other's striped yellow lips, they felt like familiar lovers again.

After Michael and Wendy gave Matthew a bath, they decided to make a quick and quiet exit out the back door and leave Salm alone with her new love. They were glad they caught Sylvia as she was dragging up the back steps.

"Not now, Syl," Michael laughed. "Salm's got a hot one in there."

Wendy handed Matthew to Sylvia, who tried to balance the baby comfortably against her pelvis. "We'll explain upstairs." The women followed Michael into his apartment. At nightfall, they pressed their faces to Michael's living room window and watched Salm and Luke walk down the street carrying a basket of the scarves she painted that afternoon.

# XV

Luke didn't often talk to strangers, and two women at the laundromat came up to ask Salm about the scarves she was pushing into the stainless steel dryers. "This is much too public an effort for my tastes," he said.

"Sometimes people want to buy them right here," Salm said proudly. Luke handed her change, and she turned the knob to "HIGH."

"What's the point of this again?" he asked.

"To heat set the paint," Salm answered while Luke fondled a silk scarf smeared with a purple and orange DNA rendition.

"And this is how you make a living?" Luke disdainfully curled one lip as he spoke.

Salm laughed, butting her head up against his arm. "Don't be so insulting."

"I didn't mean it that way. I like the way it all looks, but . . ."

"No, I understand. This isn't make-a-living stuff. This is for play money. Vacation money. The real dough comes from medical illustrations."

"Really?"

"Yeah. Educational stuff—for books. Brochures. You have a piece of anatomy, a bodily function, a fatal disease? I can draw it."

"You're lucky."

"Yeah. It's great to be able to freelance and not have a nine-to-five deal."

"I'm not good at that either. I've tried straight jobs, just to see if I can."

"Hey, but you're a real estate mogul. You don't have to have a real job."

"I wouldn't say I've reached mogul status."

"It's a living," she said.

"You know, I never felt particularly good about having all of it handed to me–the buildings, a couple of cars, a boat."

"A boat?"

"Yeah, how nuts is that?"

"A boat?" she asked again. Salm was thrilled. She never knew anyone with a boat.

"Yeah. A tugboat no less."

She was even more thrilled. "A tugboat?"

"My Uncle Jerry took it in a trade for a bar tab or a gambling debt, or something."

"A real tugboat? A little red tugboat?"

Luke smiled and nodded. "Yeah. And dock space."

"You truly *are* a man of leisure, aren't you? Do you like not working?"

"Well, I do work. The upkeep on the buildings is a lot of work." He looked at her, measuring the level of trust he felt. "And I blow glass."

"Really?"

"Didn't I tell you that?"

Salm shook her head.

"I suppose that's my real 'work' if you want me to identify something to justify my existence, my purpose for using up some of the earth's resources."

"A glass blower." Salm grimaced. "And you have the nerve to make fun of my fabric stuff?"

"I wasn't making fun of it. I like it."

"So what kind of glass do you blow? Like those miniature unicorns and all that?" She was laughing but charmed that he had such an unusual vocation.

"That is not glass blowing. That's lamp blowing. I do real glass blowing, the real kind." He paused and smiled. "Don't make any wisecracks," he whispered conspiratorially, "but I even have a degree in glass blowing."

Salm couldn't have felt luckier. He was sexy, he told her he was crazy about her, he had a boat of all things, and to top it off, this: a degree in glass blowing.

"I use the old beer garden behind the bar for a studio. Mostly I blow round balls. Round things."

"Round things?"

"Globes, I guess. Big ones, little ones. Round things. That's all. Different colored globes. The challenge of it is in the color and the patterns."

"You sell 'em?" Salm asked while she carelessly folded two scarves.

"Yeah, I sell some. There's one gallery that takes pity. But mostly it's my source of 'flow,' to use a cliché. It's important to me to create something."

Salm leaned on the dryer, her back against the round window. The heat pressed into her shoulder blades. "Will you give me one to remember you by?" she asked.

Luke moved and stood in front of Salm, his pelvic bones pressing into her. He mashed her into the scalding heat of the dryer. A young man emptying his washer watched them for a moment, possibly getting ready to come to Salm's rescue. Then he saw the enamored way they were looking at each other and he realized interference wasn't necessary.

"I wanted to commit suicide once in a laundromat," Salm said.

"Why didn't you?"

"I just remember something vague about the incredible heat that day." She reached up and with her small little finger dug some crusty matter from Luke's eye, glad that he didn't mind her need to touch him in such an intimate way. "Will you stay with me tonight?" she asked. "Or shouldn't I be that forward?"

"Why shouldn't you?" he asked.

"We spent last night together. I don't know. We just met. I don't want to be too clinging." Salm looked away from him.

"Are you sure you want me to spend the night?" Luke touched her chin, turning his face back toward his own.

"I suppose."

"You're not sure?"

"No, I'm not sure. I'm a little afraid, that's all."

"Me too."

"Then you'll come?"

"OK."

Salm's body flinched. "My back is scorched," she said. Luke moved to let her step away from the dryer.

When they got back to Salm's, she gathered up an old comforter and led Luke to the back porch. They encased themselves in the comforter and curled up on her Aunt Elaine's old metal glider. A storm was changing the sky from black to spasms of bright lavender. Rain began to splatter. Luke wrapped his arms tighter around her shoulders to stop her shivering. He kissed her forehead and whispered a bedtime story about a little worm named Willie, a story his mother had made up for him when he was frightened by lightning and thunder. Willie was constantly being cut in half by a bad little boy, but Willie didn't mind. He just grew a new head and new tail every time it happened.

When Luke finished recounting the little bedtime drama, Salm kissed him and turned away. She rested the back of her head on his chest. She wanted to tell him that she was happier than she had ever been, but she did not.

Luke wrapped his arms around her and threw his leg over her own. The warmth of her body passed through his. No matter what, he didn't want to let go. He would hang on for now with all his might.

# XVI

George had been sitting on his favorite bus stop bench since dawn, a carry-out coffee cup, long empty, nestled between his legs. He hadn't been able to sleep. His back was stiff. He was cold. Under his clothes, he felt appropriately grungy and smelly. He decided that he needed someone to talk to, and it didn't matter about what–the weather, cars, lawn mowers. Anything would do. He needed another voice to block out the voices in his own mind, the ones constantly bickering about why and how Gail could leave.

He decided to walk over to Luke's. Luke wouldn't ask questions about where George had been, what he had been doing, or thinking. George didn't want concern or analysis. He just wanted contact, and Luke could give him that.

As he approached Luke's apartment, George looked up at the second story windows of the house across the street, the house where Mitch lived, and nodded a grim hello to the glass. George briefly thought about stopping in to see him. He was long overdue for a visit. But it wasn't the right time. George couldn't see Mitch in the window but assumed he was there, and he was right. Mitch announced George's impending visit through the ham radio. "Some long lost company's on its way, Luke." But Luke didn't hear him. Luke was out back, blowing glass.

"Out back" was an old beer garden, laid to waste the years that Luke had been living in the bar. A few stray clumps of grass grew through the cracked cement. Rusted café tables were covered with Luke's glass globes–some clear, some blue, purple, or red.

Luke was anxious to devote this time to his glass work. It was what he did when he wanted to think, or when he didn't want to think at all, to wipe his mind clean and clear and find a kind of stillness in his soul. Like playing basketball, blowing glass gave him pure pleasure. It made him resolute and purposeful, and it gave him power.

Before dawn, he had fired up his homemade furnace and patiently waited, content to listen to the roar of the gas as the temperature grew hotter and hotter, hot enough to melt the bottles and jars stacked around the beer garden. Amber bottles with other amber bottles. Blue with blue. Green with green. Luke scavenged dumpsters and sometimes stole glass from recycling centers. He was proud of his resourcefulness.

By mid-morning, he had shattered and melted the glass he would need for the day. Then he sprinkled the rust from some old steel wool into the furnace so the glass would come out green. He wanted green glass today, that kind of ocean green that was reflected in the color of his eyes. He would give these globes to Salm. She had asked for something to remember him by.

George let himself in Luke's front door. When he walked in and saw Luke's bed, he stared vacantly at the twisted sheets and tried to remember the last time he saw sheets as bunched and restless as those were. For a moment, he was mildly jealous that Luke had a woman hidden somewhere. There were familiar aromas—a subtle mix of perspiration and sex tempered by a clean scent of perfume, lotion, or something for the hair.

He walked back to the beer garden. George spoke quietly as he approached his old friend. "Hey, Luke."

Luke was surprised and genuinely pleased to see him. He gave him a big, toothy smile.

"Hey, George. Good to see you."

George slowly sank down to the ground, sitting Indian-style on the cold cement. Luke wanted to ask him how he was, but he had planned to blow glass and wanted to get on with it. Besides, he knew that people didn't always want to talk about their angst, they might just want to deflect some of the negative energy of it.

George appreciated the fact that Luke asked no questions and set himself to working. "I'm glad I came," George said.

Luke nodded and put on his dark glasses. They would protect his eyes from the glare of the heat emanating from the furnace. Very carefully, he picked up his blow rod and dipped it into the molten glass. Like honey, it hung from the end of the pipe. Luke blew a quick blast of air into the rod, and as the heat expanded his breath, the drop of honey turned into a bubble.

Luke took a seat at his bench, laying his blow pipe across the long arms of the chair, rolling the rod, continually working the orb with his fingertips, dipping and spinning.

"You're the best, man," George said, watching Luke's careful shaping of the glass ball.

Luke just smiled, concentrating. He used wet newspaper to protect his palm from the intensity of the heat. When the globe was done, he scooped it off the rod and polished the ragged edges smooth. He then got up to lay the glass ball on a table where it would cool.

While Luke focused on forming another ball of glass, George roamed around the beer garden that had once been so familiar to him. Now, it seemed strange and foreign.

"There's coffee inside," Luke said.

"No thanks. I'm just hanging around."

Luke didn't respond. He was afraid that a mere word or gesture could give away the fact Gail had been in contact with him, and he had sworn that he would keep her confidence.

"Yeah," George snorted, continuing without any urging. "Hanging around and waiting. What the hell else can I do? I'm sitting around waiting for Gail to come back and I feel stuck inside a five-block radius from my place. Like I'm afraid if I go past that, I'll miss her. What kind of fuckin' stupid shit is that?"

Luke still didn't respond.

"All I'm doing is sitting around the house, checking the goddamn answering machine—as if anybody's left a message—and I'm starting to drink too much, and then I go sit at the fuckin' bus stop and then I worry that Gail will show up when I'm out."

Luke felt bad. He would keep Gail's confidence but he couldn't watch his friend suffer without giving some encouragement. "*When* she comes back, I'm sure she'll wait if you're not around," Luke said with a smile.

"*When* she comes back?"

Luke twisted his mouth slightly. "Yeah, you heard me right. When she comes back. It's inevitable, you know. And you know me. I can find the dark lining in any cloud. But I'll bet you some big money that she'll find you once she comes back."

George felt the emptiness inside of him fill up for a moment or two. "You think?"

"Yeah," Luke responded.

George picked up a large cobalt blue glass ball. "Hey, Luke?" he asked, holding the big globe over his head like a worn and tired Atlas.

"Yeah, George?" Luke answered, glancing up from his work.

"Do you really think you can see the future in here?"

Luke looked at the globe and then at his friend. "It's just a little hard to see right now. But there's something there. You've just got to wait for it."

Without a second thought, without any anger toward his friend, or any feeling at all, George smashed the glass onto the cracked concrete foundation. Then he stood innocently and crushed the shards under the weight of his hiking boots.

Luke stared for a moment, not sure how to react so he did nothing but say, "You'll be all right, man."

"Yeah," George said quietly. "I'll be all right." He bent down to pick up a chunk of glass and held it to the light.

"You sure?" Luke asked.

"Yeah, man. I'll be fine. Fine."

"More than fine, George. You're going to be a father."

In seconds, George had disappeared down the alley. He went home to wait for Gail.

The rest of the day, Luke's hand masterfully shaped molten glass into perfectly round objects. Inside of each one, he searched for a glimpse of what was to be. All around him, sunlight refracted through the colored glass balls and danced across the concrete.

# XVII

Before the summer solstice came, Luke and Salm had created a kind of life together, a loosely woven one with a pattern that quickly evolved on its own. They were sleeping together nearly every night, sometimes at Luke's, sometimes at Salm's. Although they still kept their separate time (they were very protective of their time alone), they had slightly amended their work schedules and daily habits and rituals to accommodate each other's, operating on the assumption that time available for spending would be spent together. They pretended not to notice this had happened so easily and quickly. Deep down, possibly, they were afraid if they analyzed or poked and prodded their new Reality, it would turn in horror and run away, leaving them abandoned and once again unconnected. For now, they were happy. When it no longer seemed right, when one or the other became unsatisfied, then it would be time to reweave or unravel.

No matter whose bed she was in, Salm slept soundly. She never heard Luke crawl out of bed at dawn, never felt him untangling his leg from hers so that he could stalk the deserted city streets. For Salm, sleep always had been easy, comforting, and secure. She felt a little guilty for being able to slip into a ten-hour coma so easily when she knew Luke had to work so hard at nocturnal escape.

Even though Salm's presence comforted him, Luke still could never do better than a few uninterrupted hours of sleep at a time. Regardless of what kind of energy had been expended—hours of making love, hours of basketball, walking, blowing glass—he could never put his nerves and muscles and mind entirely to rest. It was hard for him to let go of consciousness. He could be afraid of his dreams.

At her apartment, when Salm was working on an illustration or painting fabric, Luke would often appear and make himself "scarce" (as he said), sometimes reading *The Peloponnesian Wars* or *Hopscotch* (he had been reading those for years), grinding coffee beans or mixing martinis, making up little songs to sing or stories to tell, and always, no matter what, watching her. It amazed him how much he enjoyed looking at her face.

At his place, while he blew glass, she often would stop by. While he worked, she would study random sections of the encyclopedia or do crossword puzzles. She, too, would be the supplier of coffee or cocktails. Or she would paint. At some point, she had begun painting extravagant body parts in garish colors on his tables and woodwork. He liked the way it looked.

They took each other to favorite places—resale shops, bowling alleys, taverns, and book stores. One Wednesday, Luke took her to an automat on the South Side. He liked it because it was an automat, of course, but mostly because of its name: "See Your Food."

"What I really like is that green stuff with the grapes floating in it," Luke said, grabbing at steaming side dishes of broccoli, navy beans, and creamed corn. Because he feared making the wrong decision, he decided to choose every vegetable that cost 85 cents a serving. Yet, he still jealously eyed Salm's 65 cents' worth of red cabbage.

"What else do you like?" she asked.

"Meatloaf. I'm crazy about meatloaf." That was a lie. He despised meatloaf. For some unknown reason, he felt obligated to tell her a simple, harmless lie.

"Meatloaf is good," Salm answered, "but salmon croquettes are my favorite."

"Horrible. I hate those big peas."

"That's the best part, the overcooked peas in that gooey white sauce." She sometimes lied to him too.

Luke pulled down on the handle of the milk machine and filled his glass.

"That's where I got my name from, you know."

"From what?"

"Salmon croquettes. I used to demand that my mother make them all the time." Salm poured herself coffee and scooted her tray along behind Luke's.

"I thought your name came from your father calling you his Little Salmon."

"Well, yeah, that's true. But my name's also short for salmonella."

"Liar," Luke said grinning, pleased with the game. He waited for Salm to pay the cashier. Lunch was her treat today.

"Really. I had salmonella. Salm is short for salmonella."

"You know, if you hadn't told me about your dad's nickname for you, I would have thought for sure that it was short for Salomé."

"It is. You're right."

They chose seats at a white table flecked with gold. After eating, Luke forewent his customary after-dinner cigarette. Instead, he gently licked Salm's fingertips, greasy from margarine and fried chicken. They were glad it was a Wednesday. It was a good day to be together.

That afternoon, they separated. Salm had an appointment with a medical text editor. Luke had to paint the kitchen in one of his apartments. Later, she would talk him into going to a dinner party at Michael's on Sunday night, even though Luke didn't really want to go.

It wasn't that he was shy or anti-social, but he did disdain group conversation on the whole. "Besides, Salm," he said while she was convincing him to attend, "I'm out of practice."

"I want you to get to know my friends, and you could bring George for support," Salm said. She wanted to meet George. She thought if she could befriend his best pal, it would help cement their relationship even more. "You said just the other day that he needed to get out, to make contact with the living."

Luke repositioned himself in his seat. Salm was determined. "And it wouldn't hurt for him to meet Wendy."

Luke shook his head and said, "Oh, yeah. That's a great idea. Fix up your friend with a depressed guy who has an estranged wife and a baby on the way."

"Not to fix them up," Salm answered. "Just so they can talk to someone new. Wendy needs to talk to someone else besides her baby."

"I'll come," Luke said. "But leave George out of it."

Michael, Salm's neighbor, was having a dinner gathering to show off Richard. When he invited Salm, she gasped. "You mean the it's-just-sex-man-you-can-touch-my-hair Richard?"

Michael beamed. "It is just sex, man . . . like in a fucking movie." Salm congratulated him on his conquest and told him she was hoping that Richard lived up to her expectations.

"He will definitely do that," Michael assured her. "He'll turn everybody's head 360 degrees."

"I can't wait for such a spectacle."

Sylvia and Armando were coming to Michael's party too. Wendy would come if she could get her mother to babysit, which, it turned out, she couldn't. And then, of course, the Harding triplets–Tim, Tom, and Tony–would have to be there. They lived in the basement of the building where Salm and Michael lived. Two were queer and one was straight and they chewed tobacco. Tony, the straight one, was bringing a new love interest. Michael's business partner, Juliana, and her lover Cleo would also be there. After dinner, Michael expected a few others to stop by. He was known for his Sunday night dinners that started out quietly and civilized, and turned into interpretative dance sessions that would last until Monday's dawn.

"The whole thing sounds awful," Luke said. He knew that he would be on display and he hated to dance.

"But it's important to me." Salm couldn't help whining to get her way.

Luke promised to mind his table manners. Salm remembered Aunt Elaine telling her, "Never introduce a man to your friends until you've made sure he knows how to eat in public and how to talk to strangers." Worry had been all for naught. Luke surprised her and did everything right. She could tell that he met with her friends' approval (although she knew it shouldn't matter), but she felt uncomfortable with the way Sylvia looked at Luke from across the dinner table.

"That shit is over, man. Your Trotsky shit is crap," Richard said to Armando.

"It is still the only viable alternative."

"Bullshit."

"Got a better idea than Trotsky?"

Sylvia said under her breath, "Oh, can it, Armando. You don't even know how to spell Trotsky." Everyone got quiet. One of the Harding triplets butted in quickly.

"Yeah, I got a better idea. How about aesthetic socialism?"

"That sounds familiar. Aesthetic socialism. I know it from somewhere," Luke answered.

"The *Weekly World News*," Cleo said.

"Yeah, that tabloid."

"You buy the *News*?" Cleo asked. "You don't seem the type."

"I read them at Salm's. She's the type." Luke smiled at her.

"So what's aesthetic socialism?"

"It's this nut case religion whose mission is to change homos into hetereosexuals."

"No," groaned Michael. "That's not aesthetic socialism, that's aesthetic realism. Aesthetic realism is the religion that was in the *Weekly World News*."

"But what's aesthetic socialism? I know I know the expression from somewhere."

"That's Wilde. Oscar Wilde dreamed of aesthetic socialism," Richard clarified with a sigh. "It's this little fantasy world where you get all these grunts, subhumans, or automatons, if you will, to do the daily grind and leave the educated class the time and means to 'live for pleasure and for art,' as the old queen once wrote."

"That's not a bad concept." Luke spoke as he raised Salm's foot to his lap. He took off her sandal and began tracing the arch of her bare foot with his index finger.

"You can't mean that. That's awful. Talk about class differential," Sylvia responded.

"Well, I don't know," Michael said. "I can see aesthetic socialism working if you make all the aesthetic rationalists the automatons."

"Aesthetic rationalists?" Tim Hill asked.

Michael answered, "It's my own made-up 'ism' for people who

work at minimum wage jobs and insist they're artists but don't make any art at all."

"But they always look really good and artful," Richard added.

"Like you?"

Everyone laughed and Cleo raised her glass. "To the aesthetic rationalists. They look good, work cheap, and pour coffee and cocktails."

"Here, here," someone replied. From his own glass, Luke poured a little red wine into Salm's mouth and then he kissed her. Sylvia watched the lovers with an odd, detached smile. Salm was in ecstasy. She hadn't an inkling that Luke possessed such a flair for public displays of affection.

When Salm excused herself from the table, she nodded her head, signaling for Sylvia to follow her to the bathroom. Sylvia did.

As Salm lowered herself onto the toilet seat, Sylvia leaned over the sink, examining her teeth for remnants of dinner.

"What's going on?" Salm asked. "The way you're looking at Luke makes me think something's wrong."

"Nothing's wrong. I'm fucking jealous." Sylvia rinsed her mouth with a handful of water and spit it out.

Salm didn't know how to respond without sounding as if she were gloating. Then Sylvia turned and gave her a coy smile, one that mixed a little guilt with very little innocence. "But I had him first," she said.

There was a brief moment of decoding. "What?" Salm laughed drunkenly, slapping her bare knee. "You slept with him?"

"Blew him."

"You're kidding!"

"I'm pretty sure. Now that I've taken a good look at him."

"Oh, my god! When did you know?"

"After you told me he lives in the old L&J Lounge, that he used to run it, you know, I thought I might recognize him. Back from those days."

The women threw back their heads and laughed.

"Why didn't I recognize him then?" Salm asked as she got up from the toilet.

"I don't know. We were young. Stoned. Over-served. You had other interests then."

"And you blew him? Did you ever go out with him?"

"No, I think it happened in the backroom of the bar."

"Oh, my god!"

"Say something besides 'oh, my god.'"

The two of them laughed again and changed places. Sylvia squatted on the toilet while Salm took her turn at the mirror, sucking on her teeth, smearing blood-red lipstick across her mouth.

"Are you pissed off that he doesn't remember you?"

"No, not pissed. Wondering though if he has the slightest recall. But haven't you forgotten men you've had sex with?"

"Of course. But I don't want them to forget me."

Salm watched Sylvia yank up her leopard skin underwear. They looked at each other eye to eye and smiled. Salm shook her head. "You are awful."

"I am." Sylvia replied. As they walked back to the dinner table, she whispered to Salm, "Don't tell him though. I'd be embarrassed."

Michael was soon pulling out his cha-cha records. Luke sank into an oversized chair and watched Salm dance. He refused to participate, but she danced with everyone—Cleo, Armando, Sylvia, the Harding triplets. She especially liked dancing with Richard and made a point of touching his hair (without permission) while they spun around Michael's living room. Salm would glance over at Luke and catch him watching her, their eyes connecting with a kind of laser beam intensity.

It was late when they got back to Luke's. Salm was humming a Brasil '66 tune, twirling around Luke and trying to get him to dance with her. He was grinning, but managed to shake her off and flopped down across the bed to watch her and her imaginary partner dance.

In the morning, Salm gathered up the mannequin arms lying on one of the tables and managed to screw them into the wall next to the bed. The plastic limbs jutted out palm up, palm down, palm sideways. Luke was already gone for his morning walk. When he came home and saw them there, he smiled. He had never known what to do with them before.

And the days (and nights) passed, and Salm and Luke's lives and limbs became more and more entangled.

# XVIII

Two weeks later, they ran into an old friend of Luke's on the street. After exchanging hellos and how-are-yous, he steered himself and Salm away from her.

"Who was that?" Salm asked, pretending to be demure.

"An old friend."

"You've never talked about any old friends before except George and Mitch, I suppose."

"I have other old friends." Luke walked down the street eyeing a demolition site up ahead.

"Why didn't you introduce me?" Salm tried to get him to look at her, but he kept his stare focused on the approaching piles of cement and rocks and broken bricks.

"I would have introduced you," Luke answered, "but I don't remember her name."

Salm turned around and stopped right in front of him. She smiled. "Did you sleep with her?" Luke looked at her, annoyed. Salm asked again, still smiling. "Did you? Did you sleep with her?" She was having fun making him feel uncomfortable. But she did want to know.

"I suppose. It was a long time ago." As they continued their walk down the street, Salm looked at oncoming pedestrians in the eye, smug because she was with a man she loved.

"So that's how it's gonna be, huh?" she asked.

"What do you mean?"

"After you dump me, you're not going to remember my name?"

Luke grabbed Salm's hand and dragged her into a thrift store. She followed him down the aisles of discarded pots and pans, crock pots, and coffee makers. He stopped short in front of one counter. "Look at me," he said, pointing to his distorted reflection in the side of a one-slice toaster. Salm moved her face next to his, staring back. "Let's make a pact," he said.

Salm was surprised by his serious tone. "Sure, we can make a pact. About what?"

"Stupid statements like that."

"What stupid statements?" Salm turned to look at him directly, but Luke turned her face back toward the toaster.

"That kind of stupid passive-aggressive crap I hate, like that whiney 'When you dump me' bullshit."

"I'm sorry. I know it was . . ."

" . . . stupid?"

Salm had never seen Luke angry before and she knew it was valid anger. She would have felt the same if he had said it to her.

"Just no more shit like that. Pact?"

"Pact." Salm nodded a short, firm nod, and Luke took the toaster to the checkout counter.

"One twenty-five," the cashier said.

Salm remembered that Luke had a toaster coated with a few years' worth of dust in his back storeroom. "What do you need another toaster for?" she asked.

"If you or either of us ever feels compelled to bring up stupid subjects again, we can talk to our reflections in the toaster."

"And the point of this is?"

"That way, it won't really be us. It'll be excusable."

Salm instantly felt sappy and secure. As they walked out of the store, she looped her arm around him and pinched at his side. He carried the toaster under his arm, content with their purchase.

At Salm's that night, they lay together on the couch talking about taking a vacation, maybe a trip out West in September. Or up into Canada. "Or maybe we should do something a little closer to home for our first time," Luke pondered.

Salm laughed. "Yeah, I don't want to end up abandoned in the Badlands."

"It could happen."

"You think?"

"Road trips have been known to wreak havoc on relationships, especially new ones."

The telephone rang, and Salm went into the kitchen to answer.

Sylvia sounded desperate, frantic, and mildly drunk. She sniffed through the mouthpiece of her cordless phone. "Can you come over, honey? I hate me and I'm drinking and I miss you."

"What happened?" Salm asked.

"Armando left."

"Oh, no! What happened?"

"He left me, dammit, and I'm the one who wanted to leave him."

"Are you OK?"

"I'm fine. No. Well, yeah, I'm OK. I don't know. But he's gone, Salm. Finally. Gone."

Salm told her she would be there right away. She knew how it felt to be wallowing in tanks of self-pity, remorse, and regret. Armando may not have been the best man in the universe for Sylvia, but loss was still loss.

"Sylvia needs me," she said to Luke. "Don't wait up."

"Everything OK?"

"No. Armando left." Salm gathered up her bag and keys.

"This is bad?"

"No. It's good. Good but sad." She and Luke looked at each for a long time, both appreciating that the other was there. "I'd like it if you were here when I come back," Salm said.

"OK."

Salm leaned over Luke and they rubbed foreheads goodbye. "I'll miss you," she said.

"Me too."

When Salm got to Sylvia's, she bounced up the stairs two at a time and pushed open the front door.

"It's Salm," she cried out, knocking hard on the door frame. There was no response, so she headed for the kitchen. "Oh, shit, Sylvia, you look awful."

"Fuck you. Tell me I look great." Sylvia was spread out over the kitchen table, her head held up by the heel of her hand, stretching her eye up toward her eyebrow, and her eyebrow up toward her scalp. Her eyes were bloodshot. Her hair was tied back in a messy ponytail.

"OK. I was wrong. You look beautiful. Pretty as a princess." Salm rinsed out a glass stacked in the sinkful of dirty dishes and fell into a chair opposite Sylvia. "What are we drinking?"

"This." Sylvia scooted a bottle of wine across the table and toasted Salm. "Knock yourself out."

"You're not fooling around, are you? This bottle's almost empty."

"Have no fear. There are many more under the sink. Californian. Chilean. Australian. French. The night is young, and I keep a well-stocked cellar, my dear."

They sat silent for a while as Salm looked from Sylvia to the window to the ashtray piled with cigarette butts.

Salm got up to crack open the window. "So what happened?" she asked, wide-eyed and expectant. "I mean, what in the world finally, finally happened?" She paused. "I'm sorry. I sound excited about this, don't I? And that's not the plan. I want to be sympathetic."

"It's OK, Salmon. Sympathy is not necessary." Sylvia slurred her words just slightly.

Salm waited for her to continue, but a little prodding was needed. "So?" she asked again.

"Well," Sylvia began. She hiccuped. "We were just finished with dinner and then outta nowhere, outta the blue, Armando looks at me and says he's moving out. Just like that. I don't know. No discussion. No notice. No nothing."

"Well, you guys haven't been happy."

"That is not the point!" Sylvia answered angrily, then she paused. "Happy or no happy. I didn't see it coming, and I think I'm in shock."

"You were eventually going to end it."

"When? When was I going to get my shit together to do that? All of you guys used to laugh. But you didn't understand. I couldn't do it.

I was so afraid of being alone again, you know? I had been alone for so long. Well, not that long, but I didn't want to be that way again. And that sounds so pathetic. I don't know. I did love him in a way . . . when I wasn't with him."

Both women smiled.

"You just loved the concept of him?" Salm asked.

"Yeah, that's it—the concept."

"And now he's gone physically *and* conceptually."

"Yup."

"And next?"

"He told me he'd call to tell me when he was coming back for his stuff." The two women sat quietly for a few moments. "Probably there's someone else," Sylvia thought out loud. "I don't think he'd just move out without someone else in the wings." She swirled the warm wine around her mouth.

"No, that's not true, Sylvia. He loved you."

"No, he didn't."

"In his own way he did."

"Which way is that? He loved 'the concept' of me?" Salm didn't answer. Both women gulped their wine. "I mean, I was willing to settle for a body. How fucking stupid can you be?"

"We've all done that, Syl."

"It's going to be hard though. Starting over again is going to be so fucking hard."

"Christ. One body isn't even cold, and you're thinking about the next one?"

"Why not? Right now I feel pathetic. Like a loser. But tomorrow, who knows?"

"You're right. Tomorrow you'll be a new person. Hung over but new."

Salm got up and gave her friend a long, hard hug. "The night is young. Let us celebrate your new freedom."

Sylvia went into the living room and flipped through a stack of 45s that sat next to her vintage Admiral Hi-Fi. She always chose the same old favorites when she was feeling sappy and sad. She loaded the spindle, turned it on, and slow danced back into the kitchen. Salm poured more wine, and they started to belt out "You Don't Have To Say You Love Me," along with Dusty Springfield. Sylvia sang with perfect pitch soulfulness. Salm was off key.

"Does Luke tell you he loves you, Salm?"

Salm's smile disappeared.

"Well, does he?

"No, but he told me he was crazy about me."

"But you gotta get the love words, Salm."

"Well, Sylvia," Salm philosophized, "sometimes the L-word is un-speakable."

Sylvia lit another cigarette. "Yeah. Right. There's some wisdom passed down from the ancients: 'Do not speak the great and powerful L-word.'"

"There's something to that." Salm thought for a moment. Some-times it was true. She had seen it happen. Once it was spoken, Love didn't always approve of the sound of its own name. It was as if the mere utterance, the formation of that one syllable created expectations so vast and unobtainable that it frightened itself and disappeared.

Sylvia turned her head to look out the window. The wine was shortening her attention span by the minute. "Hey, look at that guy. You see him down there?"

"Look at who?" Salm got up to see who she was pointing at.

"That guy. See the guy at the bus stop?"

Salm nodded.

"You know something about him, Salm?"

"No. What?" She smiled at Sylvia, exposing red wine stains on the enamel of her front teeth.

"He's there almost every damned night. How 'bout that? And some-times in the morning too." Sylvia sipped on more wine. "You know what?"

"What?"

"He never gets on the bus."

"No?"

"Never. He's lonely, that's what I think."

"You gonna ask him to move in with you?"

"Fuck you." Sylvia laughed and scratched at her breast.

"But wait. Before you ask him to move in, maybe you ought to ask him if he wants a blow job. See if you like him first."

"Fuck you again." Sylvia got up and tapped on the window. "Hey, you, you down there! Want a blow job?"

"That'll work. That's usually the best way to start a relationship," Salm said.

Sylvia thought about it for a moment. "Nah, too much commitment."

The women laughed. The records kept playing, and they kept singing. The melodies and bass lines melted into the traffic noises and faraway rumblings of the elevated trains. Wine and more wine. Their eyelids drooped, their mouths and arms and legs took on sluggish personalities.

"So, d'ja ever tell Luke I blew him?" Sylvia chuckled and drooled wine onto the front of her shirt. "Well, did ja?"

"No."

"Why not?"

"You told me not to."

"You think you'll ever tell him anyway?"

"Probably."

Sylvia's dog trotted into the kitchen and nudged her leg. He needed to go outside. "Fuck," was Sylvia's response as the two women dragged themselves out of their chairs. Outside, the night air was cool and moist. They walked down the street leaning into each other, straggling behind Sylvia's dog, Mr. Tomato, who was seeking out just the right trees and shrubbery.

As they approached the man at the bus stop, Salm spoke in a loud, drunken whisper while she poked Sylvia in the ribs. "Hey, Syl, there's that guy." Sylvia raised her index finger to shush her. "Go ask him if he wants a blow job, Syl. C'mon." The women curled around each other, drunk and happy.

They didn't notice that the dog went up to the man and nuzzled against his hand. About half way down the block, they realized Mr. Tomato wasn't with them, and Sylvia turned around. "C'mere, boy," she commanded. "C'mere!"

# XIX

George raised his fingers to the dog's snout to gain some trust. He let the dog smell him.

"C'mon, Tomatohead!" Sylvia shouted again.

Like Sylvia and Salm, George was slightly drunk, not from red wine, but from beers and a few shots of bourbon at the tavern on the corner. He had been going there every other day—one day to drink, one day to recover.

"C'mere, boy!" The dog lost interest in George. George watched the women stumble down the street and the dog faithfully trotting after them. He wished he had a dog. "But you don't have shit," he said aloud. He laughed bitterly to himself.

He and his wife were going to get a dog, right after they got married. They had a plan to do the whole thing—marriage, house, dog, child, college fund, pension plan. He recalled their trip to the humane society. It had been a beautiful autumn day. Their application for adoption was denied because the counselor felt they wouldn't be able to give the dog enough attention, since they both worked. George remembered his wife's tears and anger as the counselor slashed a big red "X" across the four-page application form.

Two days later, his wife went to visit the puppy they couldn't have. It was gone. An attendant said that a decision was made to put the dog to sleep.

George felt a dull pain in his back. Too many nights had been spent perched on a bar stool. He stretched and rolled over on his back. The sky was black beyond the white glare of the street light. Only a few stars were visible in the urban sky.

"Life goes on," he whispered. That's what he told his wife after the puppy execution. "On and on." She had married him and vowed that she would never leave him. He remembered how they would lie in bed after making love, creating the grandest of Holy Grail stories, recounting the trials and tribulations of the sperm's diligent trek, advancing, retreating, waiting for the right moment to light the spark of life. Night after night, he would hold her small, frail body. Together, they would fall asleep dreaming of a child, full of hope and possibilities. He remembered how her breath would feel warm against his cheek.

A few hundred miles away, Gail too was thinking about George. She was lying in cool grass, watching the stars and rubbing her hands over her expanded belly. She had been gone more than three months now, had visited an old roommate in New York, spent time alone in Maine. Her sister was right. Gail always was a "bolter." When her life got confusing or out of control or too in control, it was not uncommon for her—even when she was an adolescent—to put her tooth brush in her bag and leave for a point (or points) unknown. She got a clearer head when she was out of her normal realm, when she could see things from a different angle and skew.

Now she was staying with a friend in Southern Indiana—Paula, an old roommate, a mom to four children, a woman who loved being a mom and actually flourished amid the chaos and unrelenting demands of parenthood.

"You're such a perfect mother, Paula."

"You're easily fooled. I make it up as I go along."

"But you're so natural at it, and I feel so, so . . ."

"Terrified?"

"No, not terrified."

"Well, you should be terrified. You're pregnant and you've left your husband. Your life as you always knew it is over."

"I haven't really left him, as if I'm never going back."

"Then why did you leave? You shouldn't have left unless you meant it."

Gail was quiet. "Maybe I am terrified. But no, that's not it. I guess I'm just perplexed."

Paula laughed at her. "Perplexed? That doesn't sound serious enough."

"I don't know how to explain it. It's just that . . ." Gail sighed and shrugged her shoulders. "If I'm not the old me anymore, will George still love me? Will he love the me that's becoming a mother? I don't want to feel so different inside."

"But you are different. You'll never be the same. Children change you. When you have something, it makes you different. The same way the absence of something makes a difference too."

"But what about me? What happens to me? The old me? Does she disappear completely?"

"Who knows? You're making a choice. That's what we do in our lives. Right now, you happen to be changing into a mom." Paula squeezed Gail's hand. "And you're going to love it."

Gail felt less disheartened and less afraid day by day. Something else was growing inside of her, right next to the baby. It was a kind of confidence, something that reassured her she was set on the right course. She knew without a doubt that she wanted a family more than anything. She didn't know why and it didn't seem to matter. But then the baby would move and she would feel like a coward again. Only two more months to go.

She tried to twist her wedding band around her swollen finger. "Oh, George," she said to one particular bright star in the sky. "I'm sorry." She closed her eyes tight and wished that the star would take her apology, make it as big and resplendent as it needed to be, and deliver it to George, wherever he might be, whatever he might be doing, and make him understand, make him forgive her for leaving and want to hold her again. Luke had told her how much George was hurting and that he had become different and empty. She was nearly crippled by the guilt, but she had to keep her distance until she was ready.

"You and your dad," she whispered to the baby. "You made me not me anymore." The baby moved inside of her. Gail focused on the steady rhythm of her breathing. The sky and stars seemed to swell above her, then withdraw, with the same beat. "But it's time. It's time for me to be someone else."

Back in Chicago, George stared up at the sky. One star was particularly bright. It seemed to flash once and then went back to its mere flickering. A gang of five small boys, not much more than twelve years old walked by. They eyed George with interest and tried to look tough. He smiled at them and said "Hey."

"What up?" responded one of the boys.

George wondered if they were the ones responsible for the patches of graffiti painted on the bench, especially the blue swirling lettering that looked as if it spelled out the word DAD.

# XX

Salm and Sylvia met Wendy at "The Cup." When the waitress took their orders, Salm groaned, "Water, water. Just bring us pitchers of water." Sylvia begged, "And pitchers of coffee."

"It's certainly hellish to see you two like this," Wendy tsked tsked them, somewhat envious that her child and the responsibilities of motherhood kept her from the girls-night-out drunken stupors.

Salm vowed, "I'll never drink again," and contemplated lighting a cigarette but her heart was still pounding hard from too many cigarettes the night before. Sylvia was able to lift a cigarette to her mouth though. "I can't believe you can even think about smoking," Salm said to her. Sylvia shrugged and lit up.

Wendy waved her hand in front of her face, fending off the fresh puffs of smoke. "So why the binge last night?" she asked.

"You're not gonna believe this one, Wen."

"What happened?"

"Armando's gone."

"No way!" she said, her eyes saucered. "Congratulations, my friend and newly sane one! What finally brought you to your senses?"

"Nothing brought me to my senses. They're still out in space somewhere. Armando's the one who dumped me. How about that?" Sylvia made a face at her.

Wendy was still stunned. "What in the world fucking happened?" she asked again, loudly and dramatically. The people in the next booth looked at her with reproach.

While Sylvia recounted the previous day's scene with Armando, Salm began to daydream, her thoughts wandering to Luke. She had called him from Sylvia's around one in the morning to say that she was going to spend the night there. He had sounded disappointed and lonely. Now, she ached for him. It wasn't a sexual ache, but it was an ache filled with longing. She loved him and craved to know if he, in turn, loved her.

When Sylvia finished with her story, Wendy told her, "All I can say is congratulations again, girlfriend. It doesn't matter who left who. Just be glad it's over and done with. You're too smart, too attractive, and too everything to have been in such a shit situation."

"Oh, Lord, what is it that I have done?" Sylvia asked, in a Southern drawl, her eyes focused up on the ceiling, her hands folded in supplication. "Am I doomed to eternal suffering and ridiculously absurd relationships?" There was silence. "Lord? Lord? Give me a sign, Lord!" They were all laughing as the waitress settled plates, syrup, and hot sauce onto their table.

While they ate, Salm and Sylvia patiently listened to Wendy go on in great detail about her son Matthew's feat earlier in the morning. He had pointed out the window and made a sound that almost could have been a word, or maybe more than one word. "I'm sorry," she said, finally realizing that she was monopolizing the conversation. "I don't want to talk about him all the time, but I can't help it." Salm and Sylvia smiled at her through their bloodshot eyes. Then Wendy pulled a letter out of her diaper bag. It was from Claire.

"Neat stamps, huh?" She passed around the envelope postmarked from Greece. "She doesn't really say much about her travels, except that the beaches are beautiful, and the water is always that incredible shade of blue." Salm and Sylvia looked briefly at the stamps. Wendy was busy flipping through pages of the letter. "Wait. I'll find it." Whenever Claire traveled she sent her friends long, involved, and rambling letters for them to read together at the diner. "It'll be like I'm there with you," she would always say. "And you're with me."

"Oh, my gosh," Wendy said, still leafing through the white lined pages. "It goes on forever. Wait. Here it is. Listen to this part. It's hilarious." Wendy read aloud in a tiny, silly voice: "*I'm beginning to believe in those greeting cards sentiments–'Today is the first day of the rest of your life,' 'Be happy,' 'Love just is,' 'Happiness is a warm hug.'*"

"Oh, our poor Claire," Sylvia said, putting her head in her hands. "She's gone over the edge."

"Wait. There's more. That part was funny. But wait. Here's the part I really wanted. Listen to this." Wendy continued to read, this time in a quiet, sincere tone: "*I've never quite accepted the simplicity and complexity of it before, but for the first time I'm realizing that I will not be able to experience everything that life has to offer. I'm going to have to make some choices. I won't be able to have everything.*" Wendy glanced up at her friends and went on. "*Seriously, I always thought that I could be 'me'–the ridiculous, the romantic, and the truly divine me (ha ha)– up until a particular time, and then one day, WHAM! I would begin to do what is expected. Settle down. Have children. But guess what? I'm deciding not to.*"

Salm looked around at her friends. "Don't blame me," she said. "I haven't been doing any brainwashing."

Wendy kept going: "*I want to invest all of my energy into my own life. I know it sounds selfish, I suppose, but so are some of the reasons people have children–they want love, they want immortality. I just read this D.H. Lawrence (terribly ponderous that he is) but he's onto something here–'That she bear children is not a woman's significance. But that she be herself, that is her supreme and risky fate.' Isn't that a beautiful thing to consider? Is a woman's most creative and important act to create a child? For some, possibly. For me, I think not. I have the choice (which is both a blessing and a curse) to discover what will make, for me, a full life. That will include certain things and not include others.*"

Salm and Sylvia watched Wendy slowly fold up the letter. "So what do you think about that?" she asked.

"She must have met a Greek fisherman," Sylvia answered.

"With a big one," Salm added, "who already has a wife and twelve kids."

Wendy's smiled disappeared. "It's not funny though. She sounds so awful, so sickenly selfish."

"I prefer the word self-aware," Salm chided.

"No, I'm not talking about you, Salm. You decided so long ago not to have a kid that this isn't even applicable."

"Why not?"

"It doesn't seem wrong for you. It seems wrong for Claire."

"You can't know that. How can you even sit there and think you know what's right and wrong for Claire?"

Wendy stared into her coffee cup. "You're right. I know. I don't like it, but you're right."

"How long have you really been determined not to have a kid, Salm?" Sylvia asked.

"'Determined not to have a kid' is not the right phrase. I was never 'determined' not to have a child, I just knew I never wanted one. I've told you that before. I knew since grade school. And then the decision was totally reaffirmed when we were in our twenties, I guess. All these women, girls really, who were having kids seemed so weird to me. That they wanted to be mothers was so weird. But that was their business. Not mine."

"Fuck you," Wendy said. There was nothing but good nature in their use of profanities.

"I'm not talking about you, asshole. At least you waited."

"But I didn't wait by choice," Wendy said. "I couldn't find a sperm provider. Otherwise, I would have been one of those weird 21 year olds and have had five kids by now."

"Lord help us."

"Fuck you again."

Salm took another bite of her breakfast. "But you know? The older I get, the more I know that I followed the right course. I've still never had any longing for a child."

"Never?"

"No, never. And it feels absolutely natural to be without one. For me it's what's natural."

Wendy struggled with Salm's last comment. Finally she asserted, "But it's *not* natural. It's not why we're here."

"Oh Christ, Wendy," Salm answered. "Like Aunt Elaine used to say, 'If it were a biological necessity for women to have children, they would die from not giving birth.'"

Sylvia toasted her coffee cup with Salm's.

"What's with the toasting?" Wendy asked. "I thought you were going to be one of us."

"Us?" Sylvia asked.

"Me, rather. A mother."

"I don't know either, Wen. I've always been ambivalent about it. But it seems to me that I'm drifting toward childlessness. The longer I don't have children in my life, the more I don't want them. Or need them, I guess."

"What are they putting in the water around here?" Wendy stuffed Claire's folded letter back into her diaper bag. "To me, always, as far back as I can remember, I wanted to be a mother. Without a child, something would be missing for me. Having Matthew means happiness and completion. Don't you want that?"

"And me?" Salm replied. "My gut reaction is the opposite. Not having a child means happiness and completion."

"I cannot even begin to fathom that sentiment."

"Wendy, parenthood is good for you, it's great for you, and it's something that you should never have missed. But I cannot for the life of me think of any part of it that I'm unhappy not to have." Wendy opened her mouth to speak, but Salm interrupted, punctuating each word with her index finger. "And don't tell me that I'll change my mind."

Wendy leaned far over the table. "I still don't understand it," she said.

Salm shrugged. "Neither do I." She looked down into her plate of half-eaten corned beef hash. "But it's what's inside of me."

They finished eating, Sylvia and Salm hoping that the food would sop up the aftereffects of the wine, but they still felt shaky. More coffee didn't help matters.

"So how's Luke?" Wendy asked. "Is the romance still working?"

Salm fought the queasiness inside of her and grinned. "Yeah. I'm still crazy about him. How could I not be? Things are great." The way that Wendy looked at her made Salm uncomfortable, as if she were deluding herself and living a big lie. "Things are great," she said. "Really."

"You don't have to convince me," Sylvia said. "Maybe Claire is right. Happiness *is* a warm hug."

Salm pulled money out of her pocket and handed it to Wendy. "Here's for my part of the bill. I've got to go. Luke and I are going away for a few days."

"You didn't tell me that. When?"

"We're leaving this afternoon." Salm scooted out of the booth. "I've got to get home and take a nap. No way I'm going to be able to take off on an adventure with this hangover."

"Where you going?"

Salm shrugged her shoulders. "I don't know. We never really decided. We're just packing up and hitting the big old road. Destination unknown."

# XXI

As George leaned against the washtubs in the backroom, Luke crawled into the closet, trying to find a duffel bag or backpack or anything similar. He had to have something stashed in there. George could see only the worn, smooth soles of Luke's Keds.

"Here it is." Luke's voice was muffled. As he scooted backward out of the closet, dragging a duffel with him, the back of his head knocked into his artificial leg and sent it crashing to the floor.

"You taking your leg with you?" George stared down on the perfection of the shining plastic flesh. Luke scowled and pushed George aside so that he had room to balance the bag in between the washtubs.

"Where'd you say you're going again?" George asked.

Luke was puzzled. He had just told George, not five minutes ago, that he was going with Salm to Wisconsin. "I'm going to Wisconsin, George."

"Oh, yeah. Wisconsin, that's right." He paused and thought a moment. "Where in Wisconsin?"

"I don't know. North. Just somewhere in Wisconsin. Do some fishing maybe."

"Salm fishes?"

"I have no idea."

"You can still rent a boat."

"Yeah. We'll do that. Rent a boat. Walk in the woods. Look at the cows."

"You're going today?" George watched Luke choose underwear, socks, and t-shirts from a shelf and toss them into the bag.

Luke was exasperated by George's worsening and worsening attention span. "Yeah. Today. Late this afternoon. And I'm going where?"

"Wisconsin." George laughed at himself. "I remembered."

"I wanted to leave earlier, but Salm had stuff to do." Luke paused and looked at the size of the duffel bag. It seemed silly to take something that large. He could put all the stuff he needed in a grocery sack.

"I think I'll be going out of town soon too."

"Oh yeah, where?"

"Who knows? Maybe a little visit to my folks in Arkansas." George's parents had left Chicago and retired in the Ozarks.

"I'm sure they'd like to see you. It's been a long time, hasn't it?" Luke checked his wallet for the fifth time to count his money.

"Yeah. I don't know," George answered. "Maybe after Gail has the baby, maybe she'll end up at my parents' door. She'll want to have grandparents for the baby, won't she?"

"What?" Luke asked, turning to George. He wasn't sure he heard George right. "You're going to Arkansas after Gail has the baby?" Luke asked.

"Yeah. After. Maybe I should go before. Maybe she'll go to Arkansas before the baby is born." George looked carefully at his raw, chewed cuticles. "Maybe sooner. I could wait for her there."

"When is she due?"

"August 11."

"Christ. That soon?"

Luke left the back room and went into the bar. George followed him and climbed onto a bar stool.

Luke felt his back pocket for his wallet, and then searched his body for a familiar jingle. "You seen my keys?"

George pulled them from his own front shirt pocket. "Here they are," he said, tossing them to Luke. Luke caught them over his shoulder and wondered for a moment how George had got a hold of them. He shrugged. George always did things like that. The sound of Mitch's breathing steadily wheezed through the p.a. system. He hadn't said anything to Luke all day.

"Don't forget to pick up this stuff for Mitch at the grocery store." Luke handed George a list. George crumpled it into his back pocket. "Sure. No problem."

Luke checked his wallet again and counted the even stack of twenty dollar bills. He glanced up at George. Luke had seen George look bad— even subhuman—back when they were prone to party binges with drugs and alcohol, followed by random sex and a few hours of sleep at a stranger's. He seemed to have aged even more in the last few days. Now he seemed hollow, shriveled, pasty and formless, as if he were wrapped in gauze.

Luke felt the guilt burrow through him. He had spoken with Gail only two nights earlier, and he told her how bad George looked. "He's desperate, Gail. He looks worse and worse. You've got to come back. Now." Luke didn't feel comfortable with these kinds of conversations.

"I am," she said. "I am coming back soon. Real soon."

"When? When are you gonna stop this fucking little game?"

"It's not a fucking game."

"Oh, Christ. Forget about yourself for one damn minute. Think about the other lives in your fucking psychodrama."

"Like I'm not? That's all I'm doing is thinking about everybody else."

Luke rolled his eyes at the telephone. "Yeah, right. Then think about George."

"You think he'll want me back?"

"He will fucking rejoice. And so will I. I won't have to watch him mope around here like he's been, and I won't have to listen to you be so fucking crazy."

"I'm not being crazy." Luke didn't respond to her. "You don't understand what I'm feeling, what I've been going through," she said.

"No, I don't." There was silence again. Gail thought about trying to explain (she and Luke had had similar conversations before), but she thought the better of it. How could he understand what she was feeling when she hadn't figured it out either? She promised to be back soon. She still wouldn't tell Luke where she was. They said goodbye.

Luke was staring at George, his eyes slightly squinting. "You OK, man?" George asked.

Luke tried to imagine Gail pregnant. She had always been so small. He thought of her swollen breasts and swollen belly nearly ready to burst. She would look beautiful.

Luke sat down on the bar stool next to George. "I was thinking about Gail and how she'd look pregnant."

George smiled slightly. Images of her were always turning around in his head, especially the image of a pregnant Gail, growing bigger and bigger every day. "Do you miss her, Luke?"

Luke snorted. "Me? Do I miss her?" He thought for a moment. "No, I don't miss her at all. I'm pissed off at her."

George exhaled a deep, deep breath, and with a shaking voice, he whispered, "I miss her so much, Luke." Both of the men were silent and uneasy. Luke tried to think of something to say, something clever and healing. George looked captured and scared. "I'm not pissed off. I just miss her."

Luke touched George's shoulder. "Yeah, George, I miss her sometimes too."

George asked, "You loved her, didn't you?"

"Sure. I was crazy about her," Luke answered, fondly thinking of the Gail he once cared for.

"Did you love her more than I do?"

"I highly doubt that, George. Nobody could love her the way you do."

George turned to look at Luke, but stared past him until his eyes landed on the armless mannequins. "She loved you, Luke," George said.

"She loved me? Maybe. But she loves you now, George. She loves you now."

"You think?"

"She's going to be the mother of your child." The men were quiet.

"She does love me, doesn't she?"

# XXII

Luke and Salm took the back roads, zigzagging north and west, driving farther and farther into the Wisconsin countryside. They planned on using the expressway, at least until they hit Madison, but road construction and a sudden rain resulted in a massive traffic jam. Near the Illinois-Wisconsin border, they agreed on an exit ramp and decided to follow a random path directed by their intuition and the compass attached to Luke's dashboard.

Salm liked riding in the twenty-year-old Fleetwood, another inheritance from Luke's Uncle Jerry. "All the stuff that should have been my cousin Greg's is mine," Luke told her. "I felt guilty for so long about having it all–his share of the buildings, Jerry's boat, Jerry's car, Jerry's money–even some of his old clothes and furniture. But it's funny. After the guilt passed, I was glad to have it. The only connection I have to Anne Marie and Jerry and Greg is through all their stuff."

"And your memories," Salm responded.

"Yeah, but it's the 'stuff' that so often triggers the memories, you know? I've never come to terms with it really. I mean it's the same with my parents. It's like their immortality–if that's what you want to call it– exists through the physical remnants of their lives. I don't know, but aren't people supposed to live on through their children and not through their stuff?"

"Children are 'stuff,' aren't they?" Salm replied. "But I know what you mean. I never got that eternity-through-your-children thing. It keeps the gene pool active, if you want to call that 'living on.' But immortality here on Earth? I don't know."

"Maybe immortality does lie in the stuff of our lives, big stuff like cave paintings or a symphony or some grand theory of the universe."

"But through the small stuff too, don't forget. The kind of stuff you find at estate sales, you know? Pink satin spike heels, embroidered potholders." Salm repositioned herself, nestling her back against the passenger door, stretching out her legs across the long front seat. Luke glanced over at her. "Uncle Jerry sure knew how to pick a car," she said.

"I was just thinking that too," Luke answered. He kept the fingers of both his hands hooked around the oversized steering wheel. The windows were opened wide, and the cool spray of rain brought goose bumps to their flesh. As the sun set, they drove in silence, listening only to the shush of the tires along the shining blacktop and the rattle of something invisible in the glove compartment. From now on the days would move in slow motion.

As the car careened around a bend, Luke asked Salm to hand him a beer. Much earlier, they stopped at a convenient mart and bought a six pack of cold Point. It wouldn't be cold now, but that was all right with Luke. A warm beer and a leisurely night ride on lonely country roads always went together in his mind. He and Salm passed the beer can back and forth. They each took slow, small sips, and it took them nearly an hour to get to the last swallow of one can. Luke kept driving. Salm watched his face, lit by the dim glow of the dashboard lights. It was nearly four in the morning when they came upon a yellow flashing arrow that pointed to a gravel road. Under the light there was a sign with magnetic letters. It read "Betty and Bob's Cabins."

Luke yawned and turned to Salm, then lifted the corner of his mouth into a smile. "This must be the place." He turned the big wheel and the car lurched down the lumpy road. They were lucky Betty was a bit of an insomniac and that she had cable. She was still in the motel office, watching an old movie, eating cheese snacks and drinking cola straight out of a liter bottle. Luke was afraid of startling her, so he knocked gently on the screen door. Betty grumbled as she wriggled out of her oversized recliner. "You can knock louder than that, pal. I heard your car coming down the road." She looked through the screen at Luke standing on her tiny cement porch. Then she looked past him to his car. Salm waved through her open window.

"You here to fish?" Betty asked.

"Well, yeah. We're gonna fish. Got a cabin for a few nights?"

"Are you counting tonight as a night or are you just going out to the lake from here?" Luke paused for a moment. He was startled by the screech and slam of a cabin door behind him. Two men carrying fishing rods disappeared into the woods. "Oh, no," Luke answered. "We're not going fishing now. We need to get some sleep."

Betty eyed Luke up and down. She looked out again at Salm. Then she pushed her fat, stubby hand into the front pocket of her housedress and fumbled for something. "Cabin #9. The last one. The one on the end with the porch light burned out. See it?" Luke turned and nodded. "Three nights for ninety bucks." She pushed open the screen and handed him the key. "And I get paid in advance. Cash."

"We might stay longer."

"It's still thirty a night."

Luke thumbed through his wallet and handed her six crisp twenty dollar bills. "For starters," he told her. She squished the money into the pocket that hung over her gigantic mounds of breast. Luke smiled and gave her a tiny wink. "I'm Luke. From Chicago. That's Salm."

"Betty," she said.

"Nice to meet you, Betty."

Betty grinned and winked back at him. "You two get some sleep. It won't be easy with all these old fishermen makin' a racket. Chicago, huh? You had a long drive."

Luke walked back to the car and told Salm to follow him in the car to the cabin. She scooted across to the driver's seat, glad that she was going to get a chance to sit behind the big steering wheel. She had volunteered to drive several times on the way up, but Luke refused to give her control. Salm drove a few hundred feet, parked, and got out of the car to join Luke at the door. He fumbled with the key, putting it in one way, then the other. He shook the doorknob and twisted the key again. Salm wanted to take it from him and open the door herself, but she stood behind him silently and rested her cheek against his shoulder blade. Luke finally met with success. He opened the door, went inside, and found the chain for the overhead light. Salm stood in the doorway and smiled. She liked what she saw. There was no television—just a saggy double bed, a wicker nightstand, a card table, two folding chairs, and a little refrigerator. The room smelled like lake water and ammonia, beer and fish and stale cigarette smoke—a good, Wisconsin kind of smell.

"I don't know if Old Betty was gonna give us a room," Luke lied as he headed for the bathroom. "But I told her we were married." Salm tried to laugh, but nothing came out of her mouth but a squeak of air.

She closed the front door behind her and flipped the lock. As Luke walked out of the bathroom, he pulled his head and arms out of his long-sleeved tee shirt. "I'm beat. Let's get some rest." Still wearing his pants he collapsed onto the bed. "We'll get the stuff out of the car later."

Surprisingly, Luke fell asleep quickly. Salm took off her pants and lay down next to him on top of the chenille bedspread. Their bodies rolled together toward the center of the soft, limp mattress, but Luke didn't move. Salm tried to breathe in unison with him, hoping that the rhythm would hypnotize her into sleep. She tried counting sheep, humming lullabies, whispering bedtime stories. Her muscles ached from sitting for so long in the car. She had heard the whole conversation between Luke and Betty. She knew very well that he hadn't told her they were married. Salm wondered why Luke told her that he did.

Sure, she had had brief fantasies about marrying Luke, but they were easily dismissed. She had too difficult a time imagining a clear picture of the event. She never longed for a grand white dress and "Here Comes the Bride," people critically staring at her as she made her way down an aisle in a church. (Besides, she felt much too old and too much of an infidel for that.) Sometimes, she imagined a chapel in Las Vegas or the quaint charm of a small-town courthouse. Neither of those would do either. Quite simply, she couldn't see herself looking at Luke—or so far, any man—in the eyes and saying, "I do." It seemed a ritual that existed for other people. She wished she understood why it seemed so remote and foreign to her.

She thought again about Luke's little lie. "I told her we were married," he had said. She felt her heart race. "But I do want that one day, don't I?" she whispered to herself. She knew she wanted commitment, emotional attachment, and love. With Luke, she felt she could have that. She could hear her Aunt Elaine's laughter. "Love, honor, cherish, and obey. That's a big order, you know. I wish they'd change it to 'love and be nice.'" She and her aunt had often laughed at the language of marriage, and Salm recalled a family wedding from long ago. The priest had commanded that the bride "Be fruitful like the vine that clings to the side of a house." After the ceremony, her Aunt Elaine dramatically clung to the side of the church and pretended to be 'fruitful.' Salm remembered laughing so hard that she had to run to a bathroom.

She lay still, looking at the ceiling.

Luke snorted and turned over. He draped his arm over Salm's waist. She carefully lifted his wrist and slithered out from under him. Sitting at the window, she stared out through the green nylon curtains and watched the sky turn pink with dawn.

# XXIII

Luke sang in the shower while Salm squirted saline drops into her bloodshot, burning eyes. She had crawled back to bed and had managed to get a few hours of rest even though she couldn't recall sleep overcoming her. She wanted to stay in bed and plead for solitude and silence, but decided to ignore her fatigue. It was their vacation. Exhaustion wasn't going to get in the way. She prayed for a second wind.

It turned out they weren't very far from town. It was only a few miles up the road. In front of the motel office Salm sucked steaming coffee from a plastic cup, while Luke concentrated on following Betty's directions. Each wave of her hand to the left erased his memory of the turn to the right. She was trying to get them to Roskovich's, the best diner in the area. They could get a good solid breakfast there (eggs, pancakes, sausage, and potatoes) served all day for only $2.19. Besides, they needed to get fishing poles and bait and licenses, and Old Man Roskovich ran a tackle shop right behind the restaurant. When they got back from town, Betty said they should take a "look-see" out on the lake and go through the channel marshes that led to the Mississippi River. That's where the good fishing was–even though it was awfully late in the day to fish. Betty agreed to let them borrow her husband's boat. He was in Canada. When Luke asked her how much she wanted to rent it, Betty laughed. "I said 'borrow,' Luke. No charge." Betty was sweetly flirtatious with Luke. They took her up on her offer.

After their fill of coffee, fried eggs and 'the works,' Salm and Luke geared up for fishing. They got licenses and poles, and were amused by picking out bait. Old Man Roskovich didn't find the two of them as endearing as Betty did. Outfitted for the minimal fishing experience, Luke and Salm traveled back to the cabin and climbed into their loaner boat. Luke pulled at the starter. Once. Twice. And suddenly, the motor sputtered and started a steady hum. Luke beamed. Salm had never seen him look so happy and childlike before. Off they went, Luke at the rudder, Salm perched on a life preserver. They followed Betty's directions and headed off toward the channels, exploring the sandbars and shoreline. They never did get around to baiting a hook, choosing instead to wander the waterway. The heat of the sun felt so good on their skin. The water sparkled. Everything seemed magical, and it was.

Having his fill finally of a random cruise, Luke stopped the boat in a deserted marsh area. Ducks paddled their way around them. Cormorants circled and landed awkwardly in the high branches of the trees while a crane quenched its thirst from the shore. They could look into the water and see fish–big fish–lazily treading amidst the thick vegetation. Luke pulled two beers out of the cooler and handed one to Salm. They lounged in the boat, heads turned toward the sun, bare feet dipping into the water. The motion lulled them into an afternoon nap. When they awoke, their noses were burnt red.

Luke convinced Salm that she could squat on the bow of the boat and pee off the side. He wanted to watch her, but she made him look away, embarrassed by her pose. It was bad enough that the lone crane standing off shore could assess her bare behind. They drank more beer and continued their exploration. When they got back to the cabin, they were exhausted and happy.

The next few days brought small variations in their adventures. If they weren't in the boat navigating the inlets and river or shedding their clothes for a swim in the cold water, they were in the woods, traipsing along trails and through fields of Queen Anne's lace. Late afternoons, they took to the Cadillac, meandering around the lush countryside, smelling the thick, hot smells of pig and skunk, and watching cows clumsily mount each other in verdant fields. Salm would sometimes tire

of the scenery and choose another diversion, often a little sexual exploration of Luke as he drove on, curving this way and that on the two-
lane blacktop. Afterwards, she would sit closely next to him with her
legs spread so he easily could slip his hand up inside her shorts and
fondle her sex. They liked being "bad" together in that big car. Then
there were picnics. Or sometimes lunch in town.

In the cool evenings, they sat outside with the other residents of
Betty & Bob's, mostly fishermen—some with wives and lovers, others
alone. Together, they drank more beer and told their stories of walleye,
trout, and muskie. Behind the quiet conversation, Betty's radio scratched
out old Hank Williams' tunes and new songs by George Strait. Salm
became familiar with the livestock quotes. Eyes tired, heads a little
fuzzy, they would say goodnight and find their way back to Cabin #9
in the darkness. Their box springs squeaked, adding to the country
cacophony of crickets, tree frogs, and katydids.

On their last night there, Luke slipped Pete Goshen, the one-armed
man in Cabin #6, a twenty-dollar bill. He asked Pete if he would drive
him and Salm around in the back of his red pickup. Pete shrugged an
OK and shook his head. "Damn fools," he muttered to himself. He
didn't have too much use for people from the city, but he was glad to
take their money. Pete pulled up in front of their cabin at sunset and
honked his horn. Salm and Luke hopped in the back and stretched out
on the cold metal bed of the truck. Salm liked Pete because he looked
as if he perpetually had a secret. She thought most amputees looked
that way.

The truck shuddered and trembled beneath them, shaking and
jerking them in uneven rhythms. "It's worth it," Luke whispered, speaking
to the side of Salm's head. As the country sky turned to black, they
watched the white spatter of stars appear. Luke's index finger traced
out the constellations. As he named them, Salm pretended to follow
and understand. But she could see no warriors, crustaceans, nor gods.
Instead, she connected the dots in her own mythologies, imagining the
sparkling eyes of aliens and the bright souls of time travelers.

Luke thought back to what must have been about fifteen years
ago, when he and George were visiting a friend in Colorado. They

were always getting stoned then, and their friend drove them around in his pickup just like this so they could get the full effect of the stars. "Did I ever tell you about the last time I did this?" Luke asked. He waited for Salm to speak but she remained silent. "It was a long time ago with George." Salm was glad Luke hadn't done this with another woman. She squinted at the stars to make them blend and blur.

"You know how stoned we were?"

"How stoned?" Salm asked.

"We were so stoned that when we got back to Chicago we bought a truck so we could drive around the same way every night."

Salm laughed at him. "Did you?"

"No way. We couldn't find anybody who would drive us around."

She laughed again and drew herself closer toward Luke. "What did you do with the truck? Sell it?"

"Nah. Something seemed wrong about selling it. It's still sitting in George's garage. At least, I think it's still there." Luke thought about the last time he saw it. It was sad when something once almost sacred began to decay and succumb to the elements.

Salm put her hands behind her head. "Well, you know what this reminds of?" She focused on a tiny sliver of a star, one that seemed farther away than all of the others.

"You drove around like this before?"

"No, but it's a great idea. No, it's just the sky. It's the way I feel."

"How's that?"

"It reminds me of my first sexual fantasy."

"A sex fantasy in a truck?" Luke asked. He turned and bit the underside of her arm. She jerked away.

"No," she answered. "An alien fantasy."

"Aliens?"

"Yeah. I was sitting on my back porch watching the stars. Thick stars, like these are." Both of them scanned the sky. It was truly smeared with light. "I think I was probably around ten, I don't know, something like that. And the thought of aliens made me tremble."

Luke curled closer around her and whispered into her ear. "How much I love my love's mad desires."

Salm gulped. Had she heard him right? Had he just called her his 'love'? She looked at him, and he at her. "So what happened?" he asked.

"I had just read this article in *Life* or *Look* magazine, something about UFO sightings, they were all the rage at the time, I remember, and I started having fantasies–what I know now were fantasies–about aliens coming down to get me. I used to lie in bed and imagine that a space ship was hovering right outside my bedroom window, and I would be so scared. And I would feel this strange new feeling between my legs, while I was waiting for them to come and get me."

"Did they ever?"

"Much to my disappointment, no."

"Did you ever?"

Salmed laughed. "You know, I think I might have, once or twice."

Luke laughed. "So your first sexual experience was beating off thinking about aliens. You *are* my kind of girl." He wrapped his leg around her, and she felt his erection against her thigh. He nuzzled Salm's neck and licked the folds of her ear. They kissed and kissed again. He raised her hand to his mouth and sucked on her fingertips. "You know what I want to know?" he asked. Salm didn't answer, she was too focused on the taking pleasure from the physical sensations rippling through her. "Know what I want to know?" he asked again, stroking the side of her neck.

"What?" she finally answered.

"If an alien ship came down right now, and you had to make a choice between space and me, what would you choose?" Luke was watching her think about the question. There was a smile in her eyes. She wanted to tell him that hands down she would choose the aliens. But she stalled.

"You first. What would you choose?" she asked. Luke thought for a moment. To choose between Salm and space. He looked at her briefly, and could not imagine her not in his life. Then he imagined the velvet silence and solitude of the universe, the magnificence of eternity laid out before him. He imagined how he would search the Milky Way and beyond—awestruck and spellbound, caught in the promise of the un-known, seduced and humbled. "Space," he replied. "I would choose space."

"I know," Salm answered. "I know you would. And so would I." They kissed, lightly brushing lips, creating heavenly sparks.

The sky regained their attention, and they watched the stars. The stubble of Luke's beard gently vibrated against the warmth of Salm's cheek. They dreamed of alien affairs, warp speed travel, iridescent planets, and magical moons. They smelled the smell of eternity and fantasized their desperate good-byes to each other.

# XXIV

     While Salm and Luke dreamed of strange new worlds, Sylvia sat alone in a bookstore reading accounts of Aztec virgin sacrifice. She had surrounded herself with three reference books—one on post-modern architecture, one on quantum physics for the non-scientist, and one on butterflies. She had chosen them only for one reason. They were big and thick. She felt a need to keep her reading selection private. She didn't want anyone to cast judgment on her choice of material that included illustrations of young girls lying naked on golden altars, writhing underneath images of Quetzocoatl hovering in the sky.

     The Aztec girls were glad to be chosen. They prayed for the honor. And once the most reverent and beautiful virgin was selected and laid onto the altar, the sacrificial priest would strip her white robe from her chest. Expertly, he would slice a curve under her rib cage with a jeweled dagger, and with his left hand, he would open the wound. With his right, he would dig up inside her chest cavity and grapple for her heart. Then, when he got a firm grip, he would wrench the meaty organ from its veins and hold the heart over his head, the hot redness of blood washing over his face, turned up toward the heavens and their god.

     Sylvia liked to read about Aztec sacrifice, but only in a public place. She tried to study it, alone, in her apartment once, but it was too awful. Nightmares had ensued. She stared at the picture, then closed her eyes. She tried to imagine wanting to be chosen for sacrifice, seeking and desiring the pain.

While deep in thought, Sylvia noticed a faint male voice. "Hello there," it said. "I am a mathematician." She kept her eyes closed. The voice seemed to move closer. "Hello, please. I am a mathematician."

Sylvia opened her eyes. She leaned over her book and buried the sacrificial pictures with her chest and arms. She looked up at the man who had invaded her territory. He stood across from her, towering over the table. He was gangly and uneven looking, his white hair cut short, his eyes tiny, pink, and scared, his mouth pinched. She gave him a weak smile and quietly returned his hello. Her heart flinched as he pulled out a chair and sat down. "I just want to know," he whispered, resting his crumpled chin on his hands. "I just want to know if I'm right about the hors d'oeuvres."

"You probably are very right," Sylvia answered. She looked at the man's face, then at her books, then back to his face again. She was used to interruptions. The nutcases always sought her out.

The mathematician grinned at Sylvia. She grinned back. "What exactly are these things, these hors d'oeuvres?" he asked while he twitched his ears.

Sylvia decided to answer him quietly, carefully articulating every word. "Well, you see, hors d'oeuvres are like party food, things to munch on."

"Well, would they be things like tiny pieces of dark rye spread with cream cheese and olives, or snow peas with artichoke dip, or rumaki, or chicken wings, or . . . or . . . or . . ."

"Yes, you've certainly got the idea."

" . . . or finger sandwiches?" the stranger asked.

Sylvia smiled and clasped her arms tighter over her book. "Yes, finger sandwiches are very much considered hors d'oeuvres."

"Interesting," said the mathematician. "And something else?"

"Yes?" Sylvia asked.

"Would hors d'oeuvres be served on platters?"

"Yes, they could be."

The man considered what she said for a moment. "And also on tiny plates?"

"Yes. And also just with napkins."

"Or served with toothpicks?"

"Yes, that too." Sylvia gave the man a big smile. That was all the energy she wanted to devote to conversation with the insane. She gave her attention back to her book and pretended to read, her signal that she was finished talking to him. He watched her for a few minutes and then cleared his throat. "Here is the problem," he said. "I am having a party for twenty-seven people." He waited for Sylvia to say something, but she continued to ignore him. "And how many weiner franks are in a package?" he asked.

Sylvia answered "eight" without looking up. Or was it ten? she wondered. She stared at the illustration in the book, at the smooth incision made by the high priest. The virgin's breasts were small and round, their nipples hard and brown.

"Well, now, if I cut eight hot dogs in two, I would have sixteen pieces for hors d'oeuvres. Yes?" The man waited again for Sylvia to answer, but she still pretended to read. "Yes, that is what I would have. I would have sixteen hors d'oeuvres. And if I then cut those in two, I would have thirty-two." Sylvia figured out the math in her head. She visualized the chunks of hot dogs, each with a toothpick in the center, surrounded by dollops of ketchup, placed carefully on a silver tray. "But if I have twenty-seven guests, thirty-two would be too many. I would have a problem."

Sylvia looked up. "Yes, sir, you would definitely have a problem. Because I don't think eight in a package is right."

"Should I invite more guests?"

Sylvia looked at him and shook her head no. "No, no. What you should do in that case . . ." Sylvia began, but she was interrupted.

"Excuse me," a voice said behind her. She turned around in her chair and faced a man in a wheelchair.

"Could you help me get a book on that shelf?" He nodded his head toward a wall.

"Excuse me," she said to the mathematician who had suddenly let out a startling gust of laughter. "You have a sense of humor. That is good. So do I!" He was rocking back and forth in his chair, laughing and clapping. "I have a sense of humor because I am a mathematician."

Sylvia rose from her chair and slung her purse over her shoulder. She closed her Aztec history, tucked it under her arm, and followed the man in the wheelchair. It was an electric one that made a calm whirring sound.

He stopped at a stack quite some distance from the still-rollicking mathematician. "I don't really need your help," the man said, looking up her. "It looked more like you needed mine."

Syvlia smiled and sighed. "Thanks. He was harmless enough, just . . ."

"A nut."

"Yeah. A nut."

Sylvia looked down at him in his wheelchair and felt uncomfortable, so she leaned her back against the wall and slid down, taking a cross-legged seat on the floor. From this new position, she was able to size him up. Sylvia found him attractive. His eyes were dark and surrounded by sunbursts of laugh lines. She wondered how he had come to paralysis. His legs appeared thin and frail under his faded jeans.

He was stunned by her decision to plop down next to him. He assumed she would have walked away, taken advantage of the ruse, and bolted from both him and the crazy man. He liked it that she was so tall. Her legs were limber and at ease in their coiled up position.

"I attract nuts. Always have," Sylvia said.

"Thanks. Does that imply me?"

"Oh, no. I'm sorry. I just mean . . ."

"Certain people do, you know. They have some kind of vulnerability radiating from them."

"Do I?"

"No, I don't get it from you. But you must have it. I get in the same situation all the time. But I figure it's because I'm in this chair. The schizoids, the lonely, whoever, they figure I wouldn't mind the attention, don't have anyone else to talk to."

"Well, thanks for jumping in there. You know, sometimes I don't mind. But sometimes . . ."

"What were you reading?" He nodded his chin toward her book. She had been clutching it to her chest.

"Oh, just some historical something."

He twisted his head to read the spine. "*Ancient Sacrificial Rites of the Aztecs.* Are you a student? A teacher?"

"No, just a . . ."

"Sick-o?"

Sylvia laughed. "Yeah. That's about right."

"So tell me about the Aztecs."

"Really?"

"Yeah. I don't know shit about Aztec sacrifice."

"That's good." Sylvia uncurled her legs and stood up. "But how about some coffee with the gore?"

He smiled at her. "Sure."

"And I'm Sylvia."

"Reed."

"Hello, Reed."

"Hello, Sylvia."

She shortened her usually long strides to keep pace with his slow moving chair. They hesitantly maneuvered their way through the aisles of books until they reached the bookstore's coffee concession. "I'll get the coffee," Sylvia said. "Cream or sugar?"

"Black. I'll get a table."

While Sylvia ordered, Reed parked his chair at a table in the corner. With his forearm, he cleared the table of the previous occupant's crumbs. He had never so easily made a connection with a woman. He was nervous. He thought she was beautiful, and he was afraid to think that she was only pitying him.

Sylvia beamed as she approached the table with two mugs of coffee. Careful not to spill, she sat down and set the mugs on the table. She pushed Reed's cup over to him and looked directly into his eyes. She was absolutely smitten. She had to fight the urge to stand up and wrap her arms around him.

Reed looked down into his coffee.

"Was that bad?" she asked. "What I just did?"

He looked up at her. "What did you do?"

"Oh, I don't know. Did I just look at you weird?"

"No. You were smiling."

"Well, I took over the whole situation and got the coffee, like you couldn't have handled it."

"No, you didn't. It was easier that you got it. That doesn't bother me." He paused. "Situations vary. But everything's fine."

"Let me know if I do–or start to do–something stupid. I don't want to."

He almost touched her hand. "OK. I'll let you know. But so far, so good."

"Are you sure?"

"Yeah," he said. "This is good."

"Good."

"That's good."

"Yeah. That's good."

# XXV

There had been a spectacularly garish lavender and pink sunset. George sat at the bus stop and watched the blazing colors melt slowly into the deep purple glow of summer dusk. The city seemed particularly quiet. Behind him, a man/woman/baby/baby stroller unit passed by. He turned his head and let his eyes linger on their silhouette as it disappeared down the street. He crossed and uncrossed his legs. He wanted to scream out. He wanted to sob and to bellow, to wail primal screams and groan and whimper and smash his angry fists through the cement that rose up around him. But he couldn't do that. So, he sat and crossed and uncrossed his legs, waiting for his pain to subside.

A bus pulled up to the curb to let an old woman disembark. She limped down the steep stairs, carrying a three-legged cane over her wrist. George watched her. She puffed and wheezed, her weight heavy on her swollen ankles that were thick with soft flesh and purple veins. She stood in front of George and caught her breath. As the bus lurched away, its exhaust fumes devoured the two of them in a cloud of purple gas. The woman smiled. "It's a lovely evening, isn't it?"

George stared at the sagging folds of skin on her neck. He forced a grin, dug his fingernails into his clenched palms, and answered in a controlled voice. "Yes, it is a lovely night, isn't it?"

The woman looked up and down the dark, deserted street, took a deep breath, and slowly began making her way toward home, her bowed legs carrying her bulk with uneven, reeling steps.

George had never felt such hurt and emptiness grow inside of him, and it wasn't getting better, as he had anticipated. He thought he would eventually get used to the idea that Gail was gone, that the mourning period would pass, and she would become a harmless phantom of his memory. Instead, the sorrow flourished and grew strong. Gail's and the baby's ghosts were becoming more real. He wanted to hate her, but he could not. His love for her thrived as much as his sorrow did.

George hunched over, resting his elbows on his knees, and bowed his head in his hands. He listened to the quiet hum of the city.

Buses came and went. George finally got up and went toward home. He walked slowly, remembering how it once had been so easy and good to share a simple thing like a walk home on a summer night. He walked with his head down, watching his feet.

As he approached his building, he glanced up, sensing a movement at the top of the stairs. The air went out of him as if he had been hit hard right in the stomach. Gail was standing there in the dark, illuminated by the glow of the porch light. George's eyes went from her face to the beauty of her round, distended pregnant belly and back to her face. "I've been waiting so long, George. Where have you been?" she asked, moving toward him, her arms out stretched.

"Where have *I* been?" he asked.

He pressed hard against her, mashing up against her breasts and the baby. He rubbed his nose into her scalp and breathed in her smell, as if gasping for life itself. He grimaced from the sweet pain of renewed familiarity and sudden intimacy. They held onto each other tightly, until finally the tears came. Then they stood forehead to forehead and wiped each other's eyes, frantically kissing, touching, checking each other's faces over and over again, as if making sure they were who they thought they were.

"I can never let you go again," George said, clasping his hands around Gail's neck and staring into her eyes. "You're back? For good?"

Gail tightly closed her eyes and nodded. "We're back. Yeah. For good. For better and worse."

"For good," George said solemnly.

They walked into the house arm in arm, Gail's head resting upon George's shoulder. They lay together in bed, not talking, until almost dawn. They stared, touched, kissed. George stroked Gail's hair, her back, her stomach. He felt the magic of the baby moving inside of her.

# XXVI

Salm leaned against the coolness of her refrigerator while she spoke into the phone. "I'm deliriously happy, Syl. We had a wonderful time." She nodded and listened. "Yeah . . . Uh-huh . . . a microbiologist? Very impressive." Then she yowled, "No way you're in love already! Armando's been gone, what, a week or something?"

Luke came around the corner into the kitchen and rolled his eyes, pushing Salm's chin away from the receiver so he could talk into it. "Hey, Sylvia. Been doin' blow jobs in the backroom while we were gone?"

Salm groaned and slugged Luke in the arm. She mouthed, "You weren't supposed to tell her I told you."

"Fuck you," Sylvia said, incredibly happy, not minding at all that Salm had shared her secret with Luke. Luke let Salm have control of the phone again, then he wiped away a strip of sweat from Salm's upper lip. The summer heat had become brutal.

Salm listened to Sylvia tell her about Reed while she watched Luke standing at the back door. He had just come out of the shower and wore nothing but white boxers and rubber thongs. His wet hair dripped down his strong, tan back. "Yeah, yeah, I'm here, Syl. I'm listening," Salm reassured her, even though she had missed a few important words.

Luke poured himself more coffee and went back into the bedroom. "A wheelchair?"

Salm listened to Sylvia explain. When Reed was twenty, he had been shot in an armed robbery attempt. They never caught the kid who did it. All for twelve dollars and a watch.

Luke returned, wearing shorts and a tee shirt. He dumped his coffee into the sink and checked his pockets. He and Salm kissed, then he moved once again to the door, turned, and gave Salm a kind of apologetic shrug. "I'll see you in a couple weeks," he said. And then he left.

Salm limply held the phone under her chin. "Yeah, I'm listening. Well, no. Luke just left. Sorry. Go on."

Salm sighed, already missing him, but in another way, glad that he was gone. They had just spent more than seven days together, more than one hundred and seventy non-stop hours, and on the drive back from Wisconsin that agreed they needed to spend some time alone. They each had work to do, that's what they told each other. Their task lists weren't terribly long however. Salm needed to clean the litter box, finish a freelance assignment, balance her checkbook. Luke would have to wash the car, scavenge for glass, replace two cracked windows for one of his tenants. In reality, they both sought solitude because they were satisfied, and so satisfied that they were drained. Or could they be afraid? "Or maybe we're just sick of each other," Luke said as they drove down the expressway heading for home. At another point in time, Salm would have recoiled from this statement, feeling insecure and hurt. But now she said back, "Maybe I'm sick of you, too."

"No, you're not," Luke responded.

"Then you're not sick of me either." They had driven the rest of the way home quietly, happy to be together and feeling their connection growing tighter. Something very important was happening. And they were both very afraid.

They didn't know how miserable they would be during a separation. Luke blew glass and played basketball, all the usual things. Salm finished her work, saw her friends, and cleaned out closets. But no matter what they were doing, they were thinking of each other, reliving moments, longing for each other. "It's not rational the way I'm obsessing about him," Salm told Sylvia. Luke told George, "This is nuts. It's like part of me is missing without her." George gave Luke a knowing nod.

Seven days later, Salm found a plain post card pushed under her back door. Luke had drawn glasses and a big nose on the preprinted Abraham Lincoln postmark. On the message side of the card he wrote, "Can't wait another week. Diversey Harbor, the north end, by the stone stairs, tonight, midnight, on the dot." He had crossed out "on the dot" because he knew she was always late for everything. She decided to wear her white sun dress, one of Luke's favorites, and would try hard not to be too early.

She had to stall for time. She took a circuitous route, walking past the iron gates of Lincoln Park Zoo, listening for a late-night lion's roar or the restless squeal of a monkey. She stopped for a coffee, watched cars, and the traffic lights. Finally, she headed for the lake front. Even though it was late, the lit blacktop paths were still alive with runners, bikers, and skaters. The tiers of rocky shoreline were dotted with busy young lovers, some innocently hand in hand, others groping on blankets, drinking wine and smoking sweet-smelling marijuana. Solitary people threw sticks out into the water and played fetch with their dogs. Salm wanted to announce to all of them that she was on her way to meet her lover. She wanted to jump and proudly yell out, "I've got the best thing going of any of you!"

But instead, she walked on, hands behind her back, twisting her head from side to side, concentrating sometimes on the black expanse of water that lapped up to her right, and sometimes watching the relentless traffic that roared by to her left on Lake Shore Drive.

It had to be close to midnight, Salm thought. Even if it wasn't, she decided that stalling for any more time was futile and headed for the cement walk that curved around the dimly lit edges of the harbor. She felt the pace of her heart quicken as she neared the meeting point and laughed at herself for feeling so flustered.

She looked down at the stone blocks shoring up the harbor edge. There was Luke. He had on the same khaki shorts he wore the last time she saw him. He had taken off his shirt and rolled it up for a pillow. Salm tiptoed down the steps and sat down next to him. She felt the hair on his legs brush against her bare thigh. He turned to her and smiled. They didn't speak. They just listened to the night and indulged in the energy that perpetually vibrated between them.

Luke rose from his prone position. "It's so hot," he said. He kissed the two bones that protruded from the base of her neck. Salm groaned slightly. "Follow me," he said. "We're going tugboating."

Salm got up quickly and brushed off the back of her dress. Luke grabbed her hand and led her to the far end of a pier. He stood proudly next to the little red tug.

"Jerry sure knew how to pick 'em," Salm said, as she followed him on board.

She watched him take up the anchor, loosen lines, and start the engine. "You been out on the lake before?" he asked her.

"Sure. But never in such style."

"It's great, isn't it?"

"Perfect." Salm nestled in next to Luke as he wove around the harbor and headed out toward the lake.

The boat chugged slowly across the black water, away from the lights of the city. The lake was exceptionally calm and smooth. Once they were a distance from the harbor and away from the other night sailors, Luke cut the engine and dropped the anchor. He directed Salm to the galley for wine, plastic cups, and a blanket. They settled in, the boat slowly arching and lurching, providing them with a revolving, ever-changing view of the bright skyline and the blackness of the water and sky. The wine was red, woody, and warm. "I missed you," Luke told her.

"I missed you too. Too much."

"More than I expected."

"More than I expected too."

They kissed each other tenderly. Luke stopped. "And guess what? Gail came back."

"That's good news. How's George?"

"Happier than I've ever seen him. They're happier than I've ever seen anybody."

"And all is OK? Desertion forgiven?"

"Definitely. The baby's just weeks away. She looks great. Weird to see her pregnant, but she looks great. It's like she was never gone though. They've just picked up where they left off."

"Maybe it was meant to be."

"I guess."

Salm raised her cup. "To George and Gail and the new baby."

"You'll have to meet them sometime."

"I would like to," Salm said. She had been waiting to meet Luke's friends and was pleased that it might soon be possible.

They toasted. "And to us," Luke said.

They drank more wine and kissed again. Soon, they were making sweet and silent love on the deck while the boat rocked beneath them, making love to the water.

Afterwards, they lay on their backs staring at the sky. "This is incredible out here, isn't it, Salm?"

"Yes. Everything is incredible. You're incredible. Life is incredible."

They listened to the seductive lapping of the water against the side of the boat. "Do you believe in God?" Luke asked.

"I did once, very much so. You?"

"Oh, yeah. I was a good Catholic. I even did the whole altar boy thing."

"You're Catholic? I didn't know that."

"Shit, at one point I was thinking I'd be a priest."

"You're kidding. What happened? Did celibacy scare you off?"

"No, way. Father Bob and I used to wank off together in the confessional all the time."

"Really?"

Luke made a face of disbelief at her. "The church, I suppose, is the reason why I lost interest in religion. I never felt that, whatever the word is, that zing, from the church."

"Zing?" Salm asked. "You use a word like 'zing'?"

"Yeah," Luke said, shrugging his shoulders, shaking his head. "I don't know. Zing. You know, that feeling in your gut, or when your heart fills up, when you cry, when you feel that big something inside of you, that oneness with the universe stuff."

"Zing?"

"OK. Not zing. But you know. I would go to church and try to connect with that image of Jesus hanging there, and it just didn't work. Well, I guess sometimes in a grand cathedral you can get it, that overwhelming sense of awe, but you know, you can get it more from this kind of thing. The stars. The moon. The flicker of lights on the water. From you. That's where God is."

They lay together and watched the stars. "I was Catholic, too," Salm said. "But I gave up on God when I found out there were no guardian angels."

"How'd you find out?" he asked.

"When Bobby Kennedy got shot. No more angels. No more God."

"And you're still pissed off. Man, can I ever hear it in your voice."

"You're right, probably. I guess I am. But it's still so clear to me, you know?" Salm recalled the night. "I remember when we, meaning my family, got home from my great aunt's house. I liked to go to her house because she had this big magnifying glass that she used to read with."

"What's that got to do with Bobby Kennedy?"

"Nothing. Just a little side bar. But anyway, when we got home that night, we turned on the t.v. and found out he got shot."

"And?" Luke asked.

"You know, I still can remember a reporter standing in the lobby of this hotel and repeating again and again that Kennedy had been shot and I remember this tall, thin black man walking back and forth behind the reporter, sobbing and shaking his head. I was so scared then. So afraid. I remember my father crying."

"And your guardian angel?"

"She was my best friend in the world. I loved her, truly loved her. And when Kennedy was lying in a hospital bed, hanging somewhere between life and death, I went up to my bedroom and I told Sandy . . ."

"Sandy?"

"My guardian angel. Her name was Sandy."

"And what did she do?"

"Nothing. That's the problem. I said, 'Sandy, you go and save Bobby Kennedy, and if you don't, don't bother coming back.'"

"You're pretty tough."

"Sometimes you gotta be." Salm paused and sipped on her wine. "And when I got up the next morning, my mom told me that Kennedy was dead. And after that, there was no way I could ever believe in guardian angels, or God, again. You couldn't count on them."

Luke stroked her face. "That's a rough lesson. Finding out you can't count on your guardian angel."

Staring up at the night sky, Salm recalled her and Luke's first meeting at the museum. "But you can count on one thing."

Luke turned to her. "What?"

"You said it yourself."

"I never said you could count on anything."

"Yes, you did. The day we met at the museum. Remember? You said, 'There's one thing you can count on.' You said that the little toys in the vending machines were one of the few constants in life."

Luke thought for a moment and tried to recall. "I'm not sure I ever believe what I say. Why should you?"

"I don't know. Because sometimes you're right. You can count on lots of choices in those vending machines." Salm looked into his eyes, wanting to tell him she loved him. She thought that telling him on the boat might be safe. He wouldn't be able to run away. She cupped Luke's face in her hands, kissed him, and took the plunge. "I love you," she said. There. Finally. The words were spoken.

Luke rolled away from Salm and lay next to her, leaning on his elbow. She turned on her side, mimicking his position, and readjusted the blanket over their shoulders. They watched each other's faces while their eyes started talking in their own secret code. Luke took his other hand and ran it over Salm's hair, down her neck and across her shoulders. He kissed her once softly on the lips. Twice. So softly. A third time. A fourth. She sighed and slightly smiled.

"I do too. I love you too," Luke finally confessed.

They made love again, and the sound of the water eventually lulled them to sleep.

# XXVII

At daybreak, Salm helped Luke maneuver the tug back to the harbor. They were surprised by the amount of early morning activity on land. Tanned and animated groups of boaters and sailors were gathering, scrubbing decks, readying for a big summer day. Salm and Luke walked together hand in hand, feeling grungy but not minding, slightly smiling, slightly smug, making their way through the clusters of tiny crowds.

They headed toward Clark Street and found a diner. They ordered coffee, and it was fresh and hot and delicious. Luke still held Salm's hand. Periodically, he would raise her hand to his lips and kiss her knuckles and fingertips, never ignoring her malformed pinkie.

At other places around the city (and across the world), similar tenderness was being shared. Reed gently touched Sylvia's cheek while he watched her sleep. George lay next to Gail, kissing the back of her neck, simultaneously rubbing her back. They had come to spend most of their days lying around together, waiting, anxious, fearful, and excited in anticipation of the baby. While Richard slept, Michael stroked his long hair that was fanned out over his pillow. Wendy sat in her living room, rocking Matthew, in unbelievable awe of his sweetness and smell. Somewhere in Greece, Claire lay naked in the sun with a lover named Serge. All was right with their worlds.

After coffee, Salm and Luke headed for home. They walked while a sudden summer storm blew in behind them.

"Think we'll make it back to your place before the rain?" Luke asked.

As Salm shrugged, distant thunder grumbled, and the clouds burst. A long-needed downpour riddled the city and everything in it. The raindrops hit hard. Salm and Luke ran into the Azzazaz Vegetable Mart and picked out beautiful purple plums. They stood in the storefront doorway and watched the rain, licking the sticky juice of the plums and cool wetness of the rain from each other's throats.

Every time the lightning flashed, Salm would flinch. Luke would laugh at her. "Don't laugh," she said. "It's dangerous. You know how many people are actually struck by lightning?"

"No," he answered. "How many?"

The lightning really did frighten her. "A lot," she answered, defensively, not knowing the answer.

Luke spit his plum pit into the street and pushed his nose against Salm's. He looked at her, his pupils wide and bright, and let the words flow easily and effortlessly. "I really do love you."

Salm was jolted by the words as much as she had been by the lightning. She didn't think she would hear them again so soon. She threw her arms around his neck and kissed his eyes.

"I love you," she whispered back. "I really love you too." He returned the affection. "No, I love you," he said. "No, I love you," Salm whispered again. "No, I love you," Luke said, smiling.

The storm disappeared as fast as it had come. The lightning and thunder were distant now and unthreatening. The rain turned to a soft, summer drizzle, and they continued their walk.

Salm was looking forward to clean clothes and a bath. At her apartment, they lingered together in her big, claw-footed bathtub until the water turned cold. After their bath, they spent the rest of the day in bed, napping, reading–sometimes to themselves, sometimes to each other. Luke stayed in his underwear. Salm put on a tiny-strapped tee shirt, flimsy pajama bottoms, and white socks. They watched documentaries on PBS, one on iguanas and the other on narwhals, and then an old black-and-white Western. For dinner, Salm made cold sesame noodles. They even ate in bed, out of big yellow bowls, and washed the noodles down with cold, dark Japanese beer in oversized bottles. Night fell. They lay next to each other, heads propped up by pillows, feet rubbing feet, toes curling around toes.

"I can't imagine ever being without you," Luke said.

Salm kissed him. "I know. It's frightening, isn't it? To have something feel so right?"

"Yes and no," Luke said. He noticed that Salm suddenly seemed distant, to have gone far away. "What's up?" he asked. She didn't respond for awhile. He waited.

She sighed. "I guess this will sound way too preliminary, but I might as well tell you now instead of later because when I've not told people, well, not just people, I mean the men in my life, until later, then it's turned into this issue that's screwed things up." She looked at him with a worrisome expression.

"What in the world are you talking about?" Luke asked.

She took a quick breath. "I'm not a reproducer."

Luke grimaced, not understanding. "What?"

"I don't want children," she said.

"Wait. Wait a minute," Luke said, rearranging himself into more of an upright position.

"I know. I know we're not even close to something like that. I know that. But I want you to know now, in case you have intentions, no, not even intentions, even if you have some terribly vague idea that one day you want that, that you want kids and a family. I want you to know that I don't."

Luke fiddled with the edge of the sheet. This conversation was making him extremely uncomfortable.

"And don't ask me why," Salm went on, talking faster and faster. "I don't know why. I mean, it's possible that I have some reproductive organ malfunction. That's true. That's possible, I suppose. But before I ever knew about that, I still knew I didn't want to be a parent. I can come up with some reasons for you, rationalizations, if you will. Because my father died when I was young and I felt abandoned? Because I want to help conserve the world's resources? Because I'm terrified of loving anything as much as one would love a child?" Salm stopped for a minute and looked at Luke, trying to gauge his response from his expression. She couldn't, so she went on. "Could it be that I'm afraid of being pregnant? Worried about not being good enough as a mother, or creating some hell spawn whose mission is to destroy the universe? Scared stiff of the responsibility? Selfish? Self-centered? Self-indulgent? Cold-blooded?" Salm paused and took a breath, then answered herself. "And 'no' is the answer to all of the above. I've thought about it and thought about it and thought about it. And I don't really know. I just plain old don't want to have a child. It's not in me." She looked at Luke and he looked up at her. "There. I said it."

"OK," Luke answered.

"That's it? OK?"

"I don't know what else to say right now. I mean, I'm not thinking about kids. I'm just getting used to us being together. Kids. Shit. This is new information for me to consider. Real new information."

Salm rearranged the pillows behind her and curled up her legs. "I guess it's different for men. Men are, what? Men are less harshly judged. Women who don't have kids are looked on as some sort of pathetic pariahs or something, but men don't get that."

"I don't know. Guys without families are viewed as pathetic, don't you think?"

"No, not in the same way. I don't think they're looked at as unfeeling or unworthy. You know? Guys without kids are looked at as guys without kids. Maybe a little tragic. Maybe."

"Or sexually suspect."

"Yeah. That's true. But women without . . . I mean, I think I would be an incredibly good parent. Kids are great. Babies are phenomenal. I don't hate kids."

"Has anyone ever said you do?"

"No. No. It's just that there's this huge reproductive public relations effort to make parenthood the higher road and to promote the maternal instinct, you know, promising that having kids will lead to the path of true fulfillment, that having and wanting them is purely natural."

"Well, it is natural, isn't it? Sex and creation are about as natural as you can get."

"Well, yes, of course, it's natural. And there are some people who are probably destined for parenthood, who are just right for the job, who are perfect for it. Like your friends, George and Gail. But I don't know, since I've never met them."

"You will. You will." Luke was exasperated by her nagging about meeting his friends. "Really. It's not some sort of plot on my part. They have a lot going on. I haven't even seen them that much."

Salm looked into Luke's eyes and instantly forgave him. "But just because some people *should* have kids, because some people will find total joy and all that good stuff from it, it doesn't make it the only natural route to go. It's not a natural desire for everyone. I bet that more women than you think wouldn't go for it, wouldn't make motherhood their ultimate goal, if it weren't for the p.r. factor. There are a lot of women out there who feel that their self-worth will be negated if they don't become mothers. And they let their lives pass miserably, searching, always regretting, finding fault with God, or with their partners—or lack of partners—and with the world."

"I suppose. Men too. I'm sure there are men who don't have children who lead lives of regret about it."

"Well, sure. Of course. But some of the rationale is so misplaced. You know, have a kid. It's the manly thing to do. Proves you can get it up, that's all. I mean, not everyone needs buckets of kids to work the fields anymore."

"Why are you so pissed off?"

"I'm not pissed off. I'm glad people are parents. I'm glad my parents were parents. I have nothing against parenthood. I'm just talking about the reasons people do it. They're certainly not always good ones, and certainly not in the best interest of the kid or the world. You shouldn't have a kid just because you can."

"But it's the ultimate act of creation."

"Is it? I mean, you don't actually perform the creation. You have sex and wait around, then push. Biologically it's incredibly cool, but it's not like you build it yourself."

Luke thought briefly about Gail, her belly bulging underneath her sweater. He thought that was an incredible construction. "Why do you need a reason to have a child?"

Salm paused. "You don't need a reason, and you shouldn't need one, really. I don't want to *need* a reason not to have a child. A parent shouldn't need a reason either. A parent should just want one. They should just know that they want parenthood, know that it's part of what's inside of them. But some people do have kids for reasons. Bad reasons. Like the people who have kids out of obligation, then maybe regret being parents. And that's a tragedy. And then there are those people who use kids to try to save their marriages or add some new intrigue to their relationships, which is such a total joke, or get pregnant to try to coerce commitment, which is an even bigger joke. And then there are the people who have them because they need some kind of unconditional love object or some kind of trophy or some kind of proof of something. Then there's the unthinkable. The absolute worse case scenario—those people who have kids who are evil, truly evil, the kinds who torture kids, who . . . well, I can't even think of any of that stuff."

"Unfortunately, Salm, we can't make sense of everything. We can't make all the rules."

"But we can choose some rules for ourselves, can't we?"

"I suppose," Luke said. "But maybe not. The need for life to replicate itself is pretty damn strong."

She smiled at him. "Yeah, the DNA. The supreme being." They both took swigs of their beer. "There's still too much myth attached to motherhood, that's all."

"Hey, but in myth there's power. The suffragettes used the motherhood thing. After all, how can you deny the vote to the mother of your child? That argument worked better than the one that said women should be able to vote because they're as good as men are."

Salm nodded and thought for a moment. "Yeah. The motherhood spin. The early feminist platform too. It was about total choice—not just about abortion choices—but on the whole to-have-or-not-to-have kids issue. They were talking about the idea that it was actually OK for women to not want kids."

"But that platform made them lesbians and child haters?"

Salm shook her head. "Yeah. You're absolutely right."

"Mothers wield a lot more power, that's all. More than the childless can."

"And that pisses me off."

"It's true though. Maybe you'll change your mind when you get older," Luke said. "You know, when your clock starts ticking."

"Oh, that kind of comment gripes me," Salm said, steaming. "I won't change my mind, don't you understand? I don't think my clock ever got wound up."

"So are you sorrowful about it? Happy about it? I can't read you."

"Neither," Salm answered. "I'm OK with it. More than OK with it. It's the way I am, that's all. Like having brown hair."

"And being absolutely beautiful." Luke gave her a winning smile. "Maybe for you it's like sexual preference. You're born with a certain desire or not. Like it's already in your genes."

"Yes, in my genes," Salm repeated. "But then my friend Claire, the one in Greece now?"

Luke nodded.

"She's come to the decision not to have kids through this well thought out process. She's very conscious of making the choice, weighing the penalties of parenthood against the rewards of childlessness. It's all very calculated."

"To me, that seems weird," Luke said.

"You think?"

He thought for a moment. "Yeah." He paused again. "Maybe what's weird is that she's talking about it in such a cost-benefit way. That's what seems weird."

"But why? Why should that be weird?"

"It's a human life."

"And that's the reason you should talk about it, consider all the angles. It is a human life. But you know what? Only talking about one side–the wanting side–is really encouraged and recognized, you know? Talking about the not wanting kids part, even the possibility of not wanting kids, has to be done in really hushed tones. It's banned thought really, a kind of subversive activity. Consciously thinking about not wanting kids is not safe, it makes you an untouchable. It makes you punishable somehow."

"I suppose. I don't think I can recall too much barroom conversation on the topic."

"Parents are always painted as so golden and accomplished. Honorable. Deserving. And people who don't have kids or who don't want to have kids—they're considered empty and awful. But not having children is not the *opposite* of parenthood. It's just different."

The two of them sat quietly for a moment. "And more than anything," Salm said very, very seriously, "I don't want you to think of me that way, as a bad person, as someone without value, somebody who's not good enough."

"I don't think that," Luke said.

"Wait a minute. That's too fast and answer," Salm responded.

"I already know if I think you're not good, and I don't. You *are* good. You're wonderful and giving. I don't think you're a bad person. I love you."

"But does it change things, that I don't want children?"

Luke considered the question. "I don't know. Like I said, I hadn't thought about it, about me and kids. I haven't gotten there yet."

They sat quietly, finishing their beers. Salm was glad she told him how she felt even though a thick sludge of sadness was expanding inside of her. She would like to have had Luke for a longer time. In the past, being honest about how she felt ended things quickly, or worse, led to a slow, uneasy downward spiral in the way men in her life treated her. Once they knew she was without the famous maternal instinct, she became expendable. She became less desirable and more dismissable, not worthy. But then again, Luke had said he wasn't there yet, he wasn't even thinking about children. So maybe he'd stick around for awhile. At least until he was ready for someone else.

Luke's words brought her back from thought. "You're worrying too much," he told her. He put his arm around her neck and kissed the side of her face. "Don't worry." He kissed her again. "You don't have to do anything. You don't have to do anything at all."

He positioned Salm diagonally across the bed. "Not even move," he said gently. He crouched down next to her and began to massage her hands, pulling at each finger's joint, pushing hard into her palms.

"That feels good," she responded, her eyelids half closed.

"No. Don't do anything. Don't talk. Don't worry. Don't even move." Luke was quiet and demanding. Salm watched his face. It had the same expression it had when she first met him—mischievous, serious, a little dangerous. She began to smile.

"Don't move, not even to smile." Salm fought the urge to nod to let him know she understood. "Don't move. And don't talk," Luke commanded. He leaned over her face, dropping kisses onto her forehead, her cheeks, her lashes, and her lips. When she wet her lips to kiss him back, he shook his head. "Don't move, I said." His mouth moved to her ears, then pressed down on her neck. With one hand, he pulled up her tee shirt. He sat up and looked at her breasts. His fingertips swirled across her nipples, already hard and growing bigger and tauter. "You are so beautiful," he whispered. He put his face close to her heart and listened. Her breathing was irregular, a kind of expectant panting. He had often listened to her steady breathing at night. Now, he was pleased that the rhythm was different, glad that she was anxious and anticipating. "You have so much goodness inside of you." He kissed her stomach, ran his fingers up and down her arms, back around her nipples. She squirmed. Luke pinned her arms. "I told you not to move."

He crawled down to her feet and knelt in between them. He bent down to her left foot and took the top of her sock in between his teeth and pulled at it the way a dog pulls at a rawhide bone. The sock came off in his mouth, and he spit it out. He gnawed at the other one, soaking it with spit, growling and tearing at the fabric. Salm looked startled, then began to laugh. He bared his teeth at her and tried to keep a serious expression. "Don't make a sound."

Luke inspected her feet with his tongue and fingers. Salm pulled away, giggling. "Tickles," she whispered. He clenched his fists hard around both her ankles. "Don't talk." He spread her legs apart. "And don't move."

Luke chewed at the inseam of her gauzy pajama bottoms, his drool soaking through to her skin, melting into her wetness that was seeping into the fabric. He loved her smell.

Salm watched the ceiling and listened to the quickened pace of her heart. She shuddered from the hotness of his breath between her legs. Luke sat up and stared down at Salm. They made eye contact and flared their nostrils, still trying to be genuine and dramatic in the game. He pulled her legs farther apart. "Are these especially good?" he asked, yanking gently at the pajamas.

"Not really," Salm replied, lying. They were just about her favorites.

"Don't talk." Luke grabbed at the inside seam, right above her knee. He got a good grip and wrenched at the fabric. In three short, strong motions, he ripped the entire seam, from her ankle to her crotch.

Salm counted and categorized the aches within her body, each one overpowering the next. It was hard for her to remain still. She imagined he was already inside of her.

Luke ripped the other seam. Then he pulled at the crotch and split the material apart there too. In moments there was nothing but four strips of fabric attached to a waistband. Pieces of string tickled Salm's legs.

"Don't move," Luke demanded again. He inspected her flesh, her shins, her thighs. He kissed a scar on her right knee. His lips brushed at the goose bumps that rose from her skin, and he watched them with a curious detachment, the way he watched ants on a sidewalk, or pigeons in the street. He pushed his nose between her legs, a seeping marsh that smelled like sweet pond water—mixed with leaves, twigs, tadpoles, and moss. He touched her and probed her. He opened her and peered inside. Salm's pelvis involuntarily lurched. Luke glared at her. "Don't move," he said. His tongue burrowed inside of her, licking, kissing. "Don't move. Don't you dare move." He feasted on her, sometimes nibbling, sometimes gorging. His tongue was relentless. Her wetness gushed, then overflowed when she came.

Her back arched, her eyes closed, her insides extravagantly pulsed and throbbed. Luke still hung onto her hips, his tongue pressing against her sex.

They lay quietly for quite some time.

"And you know what else?" she asked, breaking the silence.

"What else?"

"About women who don't have children?"

"What?"

"The perception of them sexually is that they've got something wrong. Like they must be inept or frigid or something."

Luke gave her a coy grin. "Or else they're sluts and can never be satisfied."

Salm laughed. "Fuck you." They rolled around in the sweaty sheets like children.

When Salm woke up in the morning, Luke was gone. It was a great blue-sky morning for basketball. He had left her a note near the coffee maker. "Be back soon. Two o'clock Cubs' game!" Salm could work on a periodontal disease brochure until he came back. Neither of them cared about baseball, but Wrigley Field was always a great escape on perfect summer days.

They watched the Cubs lose 17 to 3. Afterwards, they sat at an outdoor Mexican café and sipped on frozen margaritas. "Do you think we're together too much?" Salm asked, twirling her straw through the slush of her drink.

"No. I like it."

"But we're together all the time now."

"Yeah." Luke scooped up a load of guacamole with a tortilla chip. "I'm happy. Aren't you?" He looked up at her with concern. "Is this leading to a 'talk'?"

Salm sucked on her drink and answered him in an uncharacteristically shy way. "Well, do you think we'll end up together sometime?"

"You just said we're together all the time."

"That's not what I meant. I meant living together, making a life together."

"I know what you meant, babe." Luke wrapped his ankles around hers under the table. "Listen." He leaned over to her, talking conspiratorially. "You know what?"

She shook her head.

"I think we probably will make a life together some day. I might put your name on the 'contact in case of emergency' line. I might beg you to marry me. But live with you? I don't know if I could handle that."

She smiled at him gleefully. "Like maybe a two flat? One floor for me and one for you?"

"Yeah. Or a farmhouse with a barn?"

"Who gets the barn?" she asked.

"You and your cats."

"You always know the right answer." Salm was wrapped in happiness. "I love you," she said.

He looked at her carefully and as seriously as he could. "And I love you."

It was a simple discussion that ended as quickly as it began. They continued sucking on the tartness of the margaritas and made up tales about the people around them in the restaurant.

"That man over there," Salm said, a little drunk, her head beginning to ache from too much sun and alcohol. "He's afraid of ferris wheels. Terrified, actually. Once, he was tortured by a mad carnival guy . . ."

" . . . one with an eye patch," Luke added.

" . . . who hung him upside down from one of the ferris wheel seats and spun him around and around and around for more than thirty-five hours."

"And through his communications with Zeus," Luke went on, "in the eleventh language of the Greptekons, he was able, later in life, to breathe under water and mate with jellyfish."

"And when he's on land," Salm said, "he prefers to wear hairpieces. He's got seventeen of them, all red."

"And they're styled," Luke concluded, "in various versions of pompadours."

# XXVIII

It seemed impossible that summer was drawing to a close. In only weeks, the high school grounds would be filled with teenagers in baggy pants and high-priced sneakers, and Luke was committed to taking advantage of their absence. He took a different route to the high school, absentmindedly bouncing his basketball in front of him. He moved slowly. The sun was already merciless. He approached the court, glancing this way and that, letting his eyes skim over the school buildings and trees, the pavement and the few people out tossing sticks and balls to their dogs. Someone was on his court. He hurried his pace.

"Hey," he called out. "George!"

George glanced up at him with bright eyes. Luke hadn't seen such a completely joyful expression on George's face in a long, long time. They each extended their hands for a "high five." The hand slap turned into a firm, warm handshake, that then turned into an awkward hug, the basketball under Luke's arm prohibiting him from completely embracing his friend.

"Glad I caught you here," George said. "I tried calling." He wiped sweat from his forehead.

"I've been at Salm's most of the time lately. My air hasn't been working."

"You've got to give me her number so we can reach you there."

Luke backed up. He examined George's face, just to make sure. It was George, but George in the new form. Luke still wasn't used to it.

"What?" George asked him. "What are you lookin' at?"

"You are so different, man. 'So we can reach you there'?"

"Yeah. What?"

"I haven't heard you refer to yourself as a 'we,' in a long time, that's all."

"Well, I'm part of a couple and we know how to use the telephone, especially Gail, I understand."

Luke started bouncing his basketball and avoided eye contact momentarily. "So she told you she called me while she was doing her disappearing act?"

"Yeah," George answered. "But it's OK, man. You did what she asked." He paused. Suddenly he shoved Luke hard in the shoulder. Loud, and using a heavy Chicago accent, he started in, "You fuck. It's fuckin' OK I was half out of my fuckin' mind with heartbreak and you knew where my wife was and you didn't fucking tell me." George playfully shoved Luke again.

Luke pushed George back and responded in the same way—loud, silly, and large. "You stupid fuck. I didn't know where she fucking was."

"But you knew she was fucking coming back and you didn't fucking tell me."

"I dropped enough fucking hints, asshole. It's not my fault you were so fucking stupid not to get 'em. You just ought to fucking thank me for getting her to come back to you."

"Bullshit. You got her to come back? Fuck you. She came back because she loves my ass," George said.

"Because she felt fucking sorry for your ass."

George smiled. "Or maybe because she wanted her son to meet his fucking Uncle Luke." George then stepped back and pulled a fat cigar out of his pocket while Luke quickly decoded the words.

A smile spread over his face now too. "No way! When?"

"Last night."

Luke took the cigar and unwrapped it. "How'd it go? Awful?"

"No, it wasn't bad at all. But Gail probably wouldn't say that. But everything's good. He's good. A new little George."

"Oh, Christ. You didn't do a George, Jr., thing, did you?"

"What's wrong with George?"

"It's just too fucking confusing. I'm gonna call him something different. Something like . . ."

"What?"

"I don't know. Sparky?" Luke wet the tip of his cigar.

"Fuck Sparky. My kid deserves a better name than Sparky."

"Voltran?"

"No."

"Thor?"

George paused. "Thor's not bad." George slung his arm over Luke's shoulder. "Let's go see him."

The medical center wasn't far from the high school, so they decided to walk the entire way. Once there, George led Luke through the maze of corridors as if he were the ruler of the universe. Gail was sleeping when they walked into her room. The baby was asleep too in a crib next to her bed. Mother and child were nearly in the same position and so were their expressions, both peaceful and beautiful. "Look at 'em," George whispered. "Just look at 'em."

Luke did. He moved to the crib and leaned over the baby to take stock of his features, every hair on his head, each eyelash, his nose, his lips, his cheeks, his long fingers, the wrinkles on his knuckles, the tiny nails. Luke felt as if he were witnessing a miracle for the first time. He was stunned by the child and stunned by his response to him. He realized he felt the way he did when he looked up at mountains or up at the sky. He felt small, insignificant, reverent. George came up behind him.

"What do you think?"

"He's fucking something, George."

"Yeah. It's great. It's fucking great."

The two of them stood silent, spellbound by the baby, intently watching him breathe.

Gail awoke and weakly smiled at George, then at Luke. "How is he?" she asked.

"Good. He's fine. Sleeping."

"Good," Gail said, drifting off again.

Luke bent over her and kissed her gently on the cheek. "Congratulations, Mom," he said.

"What til you hold him," George said, pulling a vinyl chair close between the crib and the hospital bed. "It's incredible."

Luke stood and looked from Gail to George to the baby. They were a unit, an invincible unit now. He thought of Salm for a moment. She would never be part of such a scene. He had a fleeting thought of himself in such a picture, but it was hard to bring it into focus.

"You fucking did it," Luke said. "You made yourself a dad." The friends "high fived" each other one more time.

# XXIX

Luke had stopped by Mitch's to tell him about the baby. The two of them sat together at the kitchen table. There was a bottle of Early Times bourbon between them. Mitch shook his head, grinning. "George a father. That's something, isn't it?"

George and Luke were Mitch's favorite kids from the old neighborhood. When they were teenagers, Mitch used to let them have girls up at his place when he wasn't there, and he didn't complain if there were a few beers missing when he came home. "George is a man now," Mitch said.

Luke was taken somewhat aback. "He's already a man, Mitch. Shit, we're almost middle-aged men. You're a man, aren't you? And you never had any kids."

"Yes. He's already a man. But a different kind of man. There's something about being a father that'll make him a different kind of man. You'll see." Mitch sipped at his bourbon. His eyes were rimmed with red, and he seemed tired. "I remember your father and Jerry and those other guys from the tavern. The way they'd play with all you kids outside on the sidewalk."

Luke remembered his father's face. He missed him.

"You used to play with us, too."

Mitch squinted his eyes. "Yeah, I played with you kids, but it was different. I went home afterwards by myself."

Luke poured himself another shot glass of bourbon. He could remember those times, especially in the summer, playing outside with the other kids, the streetlights just coming on, and the "old" guys–who were then maybe forty–straggling home, some covered with paint, others with plaster or saw dust, some with hard hats tucked under their arms. Luke remembered Mitch back then. He also went home, like the kids and like most of the other dads, once it was dark. Luke could remember Mitch leaving the bar, snarling something to them like, "Getta outta here and get home," crossing the street, slowly making his way up the stairs to his apartment.

"Who brought this?" Luke asked, picking the top off a plastic cake saver. Inside was a layer cake smeared with white frosting.

"My sister was here." Mitch nodded his head toward the cake. "Like I want all that."

"I'll eat it," Luke said, getting up to get a fork and a plate. "How's she doin'?"

"Pain in the ass," Mitch answered. Luke tried to cut Mitch a piece of cake, but he refused. Luke cut himself a very large one.

"Give her some slack," Luke said.

"Pain in the ass. She spent the whole day cleaning, scouring the bathroom, getting down on her knees, scrubbing the kitchen floor, dusting the baseboards."

Luke gave the room a once over. "Looks good." He took a bite of cake. "Delicious," he said. "Sure you don't want any?"

"No." The sound of skateboards and laughing teenagers came up through Mitch's windows. "Goddamn kids."

"They're not doing anything wrong."

Mitch snorted. There was a sound of smashing glass and more laughter. Luke wondered if the kids in the neighborhood thought of him as a solitary, eccentric character, blowing glass in the backyard. He hoped that they had seen him with Salm, had seen him kiss her, had seen that he was attached to another human being.

"They ever bother your stuff in back?"

"Nah. If they did, so what? It's not worth much."

"It's yours though. That makes it worth something."

The two of them sat quietly. Luke washed down the cake with

bourbon and got up to put his plate in the sink. Mitch's breathing seemed strained. His leathery skin seemed almost tinted gray.

Luke leaned against the kitchen counter. "You need anything at the store?" he asked. "I'm going tomorrow."

Mitch's eyes moved toward the back window. "Remember Mrs. Hernandez, Luke?"

"The one who sang?"

"Yeah." She had lived next door to Mitch. Her stunning voice used to carry down the street and through the alley and gangways. Mitch recalled her in the back yard, clothes pins in her mouth, while she hung shirts and slips and sheets out to dry, watching her kids run through the sprinkler on hot summer afternoons.

"Sit down," Mitch said, tapping at the kitchen table. "Sit back down." Mitch pinched his lips together. "Don't go yet."

Luke followed the instructions. Mitch had never before asked him to prolong his stay. Usually he cut Luke's visits short. Their conversations were the same face to face or over the ham radio. Abbreviated. Functional. Sparse. Luke was intrigued by the opportunity to reminisce.

They talked about the old days—Hop and Judge and their Saturday nights brawls at the L&J, the bowling league, the fireworks for the annual block party, the eleven Lipof kids—always trouble, filthy, and snot-nosed. The time Greg was in that bad car accident on the next street, the night the Bears won the SuperBowl. They remembered when the Petroski's grocery was bought by the Daoud family. The empty lot where the teenagers hung out, made out, smoked pot. They shared stories about Luke's mom and dad and Uncle Jerry and Anne Marie. Like the time they gave Mitch a surprise birthday party—his fiftieth. It was the first birthday party Mitch had ever had. They talked about how everyone was gone now, everyone but them. Luke and Mitch. The last holdovers from what was once a real, old-fashioned, connected neighborhood.

"Maybe George'll move back, now that the yuppies are startin' to buy these places up," Mitch said.

Luke told Mitch again about the baby and his sweet perfection.

"When I held him . . ." Luke recalled the infant in his arms so clearly that he could almost feel its weight, "he kinda opened his eyes and looked at me, trusting me, you know? He felt safe. It was something. Really something."

Mitch listened, watching Luke's expression. "What about you? What about you and this girl?"

Luke smiled. "Salm? She's great. Yeah. She's great."

"She looks good, that's for sure." Mitch winked. "You love her?"

Luke shifted in his seat. "Yeah. I suppose."

"You sure?"

He slowly nodded, putting his entire torso into the movement. "Yeah. I'm very sure."

"Ready to follow in George's footsteps?"

Luke shook his head, pursing his lips. "Nah. That's not, that's not in the cards."

"You sure?"

"She's sure. It's not part of her plan."

Mitch grimaced as if something had twisted inside of him. His breathing was strained. He coughed.

"You OK?"

He didn't respond. He seemed to look at something far away, his eyes slightly narrowed, shoulders hunched. He flinched again.

"You OK?"

Mitch still didn't respond, his eyes still focused on something in the distance.

Luke bent over and looked in Mitch's face. "Mitch? You OK?"

Mitch shook something off and cleared his throat. "Jesus Christ. I'm fine."

Luke refilled their glasses with bourbon. Mitch watched him pour, while Luke made sure the amounts were exactly even.

"You know how people are always spewing that bullshit about how you got to live your life so you don't have any regrets?" Mitch asked.

Luke eyed the portions one more time. "Yeah. I heard that before."

"It don't work that way. You know that?"

Luke nodded mindlessly.

"You—me—hell, nobody—can have everything they want. Or what they think they might want. Just can't." Mitch sighed and seemed to sink a little further into his seat. "Some things come by fate, Luke, or circumstance, divine intervention, or what have you. And you can work with whatever it is you're handed or you can sit there and look at it and do nothing, or you can welcome it, or you can whine about it, or you can take advantage of it. But there's one thing to remember."

"What's that?"

"Every fate possible is not possible. Not possible at all. You're going to have regrets."

Luke sat still, semi-stunned. Mitch was not one for pronouncements of any kind.

"No matter how good fate is to you or how many good choices you make, there's no way around it. You're just gonna have a regret or two."

Luke considered Mitch's words. He was afraid to ask, but felt compelled to do so. "Do you have any regrets, Mitch?"

"Well, shit, of course I do. What do you think this is all about? I regret a few things. Some big things. Some small."

"Like what?"

Mitch thought for a moment. "I regret selling that Electra."

Luke laughed. "That was a great car. I got a blow job in that car once, in high school."

Mitch scowled back at him. "And I regret the fact that I never did, my boy," Mitch said, suddenly smiling. "But you know what, Luke? I wouldn't do it over any other way, and that is a damned important thing to be able to say. I'm proud of that."

"You wouldn't do anything different?"

"Nope. I have been a happy and contented man." He put his hands up slightly as if to ward something off. "Now I know you may think that that's a load of bullshit, but it's not."

"You never regretted settling down and having a family?"

"Nope. So I never married. So what? I never had it in me to love a woman, Luke. And maybe I missed out. But I loved a lot of other things." He paused and looked at Luke carefully, judging him, taking full stock of his lifelong friend. He raised his eyebrows and his eyes glimmered. "One thing I loved once was a man, Luke."

Luke stared at Mitch wide-eyed.

"Yup. I loved a man once, when I was in the service. His name was Harold Pruitt. Don't be so surprised. But that was a long time ago and not worth talking about now."

Luke poured himself a touch more of bourbon and wet his lips with it. "I'm so . . . I didn't . . . ," he stammered.

"Not worth talking about, Luke," Mitch said, veering away from the subject now that the confessional was over. "And I loved my books. My radio building. Trips up to Ontario. My small accomplishments, you know—my tomatoes, refinishing the wordwork." He glanced around the room. "All my solitary habits. Shit, I love my solitude. But I also loved being a part of this neighborhood for so long. I needed to belong to it in my estranged way, like some sort of grand overseer."

"Yeah, you were always that. The Big Eyes Upstairs. The guy who always knew what was going on."

"You kids were always afraid I'd tell your parents if you ever did anything wrong." Mitch thought for a moment. "And I would have, if it was bad enough." Mitch sucked down the last of his drink and shuddered. "But I learned something from this life, Luke—Don't spend your time wallowing in the shit. That shouldn't be part of the human experience, if you can help it, that is."

Luke smiled. He lifted his glass toward Mitch.

"Human beings can be incredibly adaptable to the hand they're dealt, you know that? If they want to be. Time does a lot of work in this world. It rearranges our priorities and eases our sorrows. It can reroute our dreams. And if you're lucky, like I've been lucky, living in this city, with a good job, heat, food, all the necessities, friends, a sense of belonging, without horror, without too much tragedy, well, if you're that lucky, you don't have the right to store too much inventory in the complaint department."

Luke looked at his friend in the eyes. "You're right, Mitch. You're right."

"The most important thing to remember is to do what's right for you, Luke. You're a lucky sonnofabitch. All you kids are."

Luke swirled the bourbon in his glass and looked into it. He knew that he was lucky.

"You can have the life you want, Luke, and that's a rare opportunity."

"It is," Luke agreed.

"You can leave something on this Earth when you go, if you're lucky enough. But in the last moment, the only thing you get to take with you is your own life and your own memories. It'd be a damn shame not to take away the life you wanted."

Luke went home, crossing the street as the street lights flashed on. His eyes were bleary from the bourbon, old memories, new emotions. Inside, he turned on two fans and poured himself another drink.

He noticed the light on his answering machine. "Hi, babe," Salm said. "I'm going over to Sylvia's for awhile. She's had a rough day. Three funerals. I'll call you when I get home, or I'll see you at my place if you go there. Either way. Love you."

He lay down in bed, his head propped up by pillows, and sipped on the bourbon. He thought about George and Gail and the baby. Mitch. He thought about Salm. He looked around the bar. This was his life.

# XXX

Salm missed Luke when she woke up that morning, but she had work to do and that took her attention. She spent a leisurely afternoon sorting through dusty fabrics in resale shops. When she was short on new ideas for fabric designs, she often found inklings of discovery in old draperies, sport coat linings, and house dresses. She had a productive day and looked forward to an evening with Luke. He was going to give her a massage. Every week, they got to request some kind of special attention that the other was absolutely obligated to deliver. Salm liked the plan because it was her idea.

While she waited for him, she watched a rerun of a "Love Boat" episode, the one that takes place in Australia where Julie, the cruise director, falls in love with the veterinarian who is dying of cancer. Salm kept her remote control in her hand, ready to shut off the television when Luke walked in. She didn't want him to know she really liked such sentimental, predictable trash. It was the one of the secrets that she kept from him: She liked reruns of "The Love Boat."

But her video pleasure wasn't interrupted by Luke. Sylvia called. She needed her. Three of the AIDS patients she took food to had died. All of them were buried in that one day. Reed was out of town at a conference. She needed a shoulder to cry on.

Salm left Luke a message on his answering machine. She also left a note for him on the refrigerator and signed it with *x*'s and *o*'s and a deep red lipstick kiss. He would know where she went one way or the other.

When Salm walked into Sylvia's kitchen, the two women hugged hard. Sylvia clung to Salm, digging her chin into Salm's shoulder. Sylvia cried, "My dearest god, Salm, they just die and we can't do anything about it."

Sylvia reminisced about them—Les, Don, and Stewart. She talked about how charming they were, how vital and positive their attitudes were, and how they made her laugh and made her feel loved, and now she was full of pain because of their deaths, but mostly because she felt as if she took more from them than she had given.

"At least they weren't alone. They died with their friends with them. Some family, too. At least they weren't alone," Sylvia told her.

Holding hands over the kitchen table, both Salm and Syl let big teardrops roll from their eyes. They didn't say much after that. They sat and drank coffee and smoked cigarettes. After sharing understanding and knowing glances with each other, Sylvia said she wanted to talk, but not about death. There was nothing more to say about that. It defied words. It was nothing but a big black page of ink.

She asked Salm about Luke.

Salm answered as she looked inside her empty coffee mug. "I haven't told you yet, I told Michael, but," she said, taking a deep breath, "Luke told me he was going to marry me someday." Then she got up to try to turn off the dripping faucet.

"Yikes!" Syvlia yelped. "That's scary. You and your constant flow of marriage proposals. You think you'd go through with this one?"

Salm's eyes widened. "You're asking me? I don't know. Shit."

"When do you tell him you don't want any kids? That'll be the determining factor, won't it?"

"I already did that."

"No way! And he didn't bolt?"

"No, he didn't bolt. Not yet anyway. But he hasn't had time to think about it, if he has at all."

The women were quiet again. "I'm so scared he'll disappear," Salm said.

Sylvia looked out the window to the dark streets and saw her reflection in the pane. "You know what?" she asked.

"What?"

"I would marry Reed in one second."

"You're kidding."

"No, I'm not kidding. I would marry him. Do you believe that?"

"Yeah, I believe it. You were ready to dive in with Armando. You thought he was the one."

"I did, that's true." Sylvia sucked on her teeth. "I don't know. Who knows? We've all planned on a few commitments before. You pick one, you pick another. You can never know one hundred percent if it's right, can you?"

"Oh, why not, Syl? What always happens?"

"Who knows? Fuck. You. Me. Claire. All the women we know. We're so unsure about commitments and so afraid, that it's no wonder our romances end. There's some kind of self-fulfilling prophecy going on."

"Or else men can smell it on us. You know? Our very primitive instincts are still operative. They can smell that we're not sure."

"And that we're not good breeding material." Salm laughed. "That's it, really. There could be something to that." She sniffed at the air. "But maybe we can smell it if they're not the right ones too."

"And we haven't followed our instincts enough." Sylvia took a deep breath. "I think Reed's got the right smell." She breathed in deeply again. "So does Luke."

"You remember how he smells?" Salm got up and went to the refrigerator. She pulled out two bottles of beer and twisted the caps off, protecting her fingers with the sleeve of her shirt. "Here." She put a beer in front of Sylvia. "Wash the taste out of your mouth."

Sylvia rolled her eyes. "This one joke will never end, will it?"

"No," Salm answered, grinning at her. She sat back down.

"I don't know," Sylvia said while she peeled the label off of her beer bottle. "It seems relationships die the same way people do. Sometimes you see the disease spread, watch it linger, and wait for the last breath. And sometimes, there's an accident, a tragedy, and a suddenness to it all. It's always different, and there's nothing we can ever do about it."

"That's such a depressing take. I wonder if I'll live long enough, or ever be smart enough, to ever see a relationship outlast me." Salm became momentarily dreamy. She imagined a death bed farewell to a faceless lover. "What would that be like?"

Sylvia tried to imagine the same thing and then pushed the thought away. "I can't do that," she said. She took a big gulp of beer. "I've got enough bad images in my head without creating any more maudlin melancholy."

"I'm just scared stiff about giving up my life to one person," Salm said. "Always have been."

"It's the only life we have. It's a big risk."

"But, why?" Salm asked, exasperated, slouching into her chair. "Why does it have to be such a big fucking risk? Why can't I be sure? Shit. I've been in and out of god knows how many relationships, Syl, and I still don't have a clue about what a hundred percent satisfactory good relationship is. It's such a nebulous, illusive concept to me. I'm sure it's always around the corner but . . ."

"Maybe we should have read the articles in *Cosmopolitan* when we were teenagers."

Salm laughed. "I want to try to make this work with Luke though. With this one, maybe I can close my eyes and take the plunge. To go boldly where I've never dared to go before."

Sylvia smiled. "Yeah. Maybe it's time. I hope it's right for you."

"I hope that for you too."

"And if it's not? What's the big deal? You won't know unless you try and give it your best shot. Sooner or later, you have to make your own kind of human sacrifice, right? Or you'll always wonder."

They looked at each other and drank their beers. "Oh, Christ," Salm said. "I can't even think about it in those terms."

# XXXI

When Luke woke in the morning, his telephone was on his bed. He instantly recalled talking to Salm sometime in the night. He remembered that she had apologized. She was still at Sylvia's and just leaving. When had that been? Not late, around ten o'clock? She said she would come over, but Luke had mumbled something about its being too hot. Besides, he was dead asleep. He drank too much bourbon with Mitch. Tomorrow, he said. He would see her tomorrow.

Now, he had second thoughts.

Luke readied for his morning walk. He got the paper, went to the Busy Bee for eggs and jalapeños. After that he stopped at a florist and bought an armload of asters for Gail. He knew the flowers by sight, not by name. He remembered seeing the same kind on her kitchen table before.

All were asleep when he walked into the hospital room. Gail, the baby, even George, his head back, mouth open, loudly snoring, looking uncomfortable in the orange vinyl chair. Luke watched them, mesmerized. He laid the flowers on Gail's food tray.

Luke wanted to touch the baby. Stealthily, he reached out and gently placed his finger on the top of the baby's hand. The infant moved, a little twitch, a little stretch. Luke watched as the baby balled his fingers up into a tiny fist and trembled.

After he left the hospital, he went directly to Salm's. She was on the back porch reading, still drinking morning coffee.

"Hey," she brightened when she saw Luke appear. "I missed you last night." She got up and kissed him.

"Any more coffee?" he asked. He went into the kitchen before she answered.

She followed him in. "What's going on?"

He poured himself some coffee and smiled sweetly. "Gail had the baby."

"Really! What they'd have?"

"A boy. George Jr. though, so that's a problem, but he's cute."

"I bet." Salm paused. "You've already seen him?"

"Yeah. Yesterday. And I went this morning too to take some flowers."

They went back outside and sat in the glider. Luke picked up the book Salm had been reading and looked at the spine absent-mindedly. *Jude the Obscure.* He handed the book back to her.

"So tell me about the baby."

Luke shrugged. "He's a baby. He's little and perfect."

"I'll go with you the next time you go to the hospital, OK?"

"Sure. But I think they'll probably go home today. I don't know how that works."

"Yeah. Neither do I." They each sipped their coffee. "Then we'll go to their place. Wherever. We'll have to take a present." Salm tried to sound upbeat, but she was starting to feel miserable, guilty, and strangled. Luke was different. Some kind of internal voice, out of her control, was crying out "Fuck you, George! Fuck you, Gail! You've ruined everything!" The voice reverberated through her entire body.

"How's Sylvia?" Luke asked.

"Better. It's tough. She watches these poor guys every day get sicker and sicker.

"Yeah. I'm worried about Mitch. He seems sick," Luke said. He was stroking the stubble on his chin. "I spent a lot of time with him yesterday. More time than I think I ever have."

"Maybe that's why."

"What do you mean?"

"Well, maybe that's why you wanted to spend so much time together. You're both realizing that time is short."

"That's morbid."

"How old is he?"

"I don't know. Eighty, eighty-five. He's pretty old."

"Well, he's gotta be thinking about his mortality."

Luke sighed. "Yeah, I know. He seemed . . . tired, that's all, worn out."

They sat quietly, rocking, drinking coffee.

Luke sort of chuckled. "We reminisced about the old neighborhood. Some pretty funny stuff."

"I bet." For the first time, Salm noticed that the usually constant electrical charge that ran between her and Luke had run down. Now it was only a flicker, a tiny, tiny flicker.

"Yeah. I had never talked to Mitch like that before. He started going on about life, the choices we make, shit like that."

"Mmmm," Salm said. "And children, reasons for living, posterity?" She was angry with herself for feeling abandoned and alone. Luke had been with Mitch, George, Gail, the baby, and she had been omitted. But Luke was there with her right now. Wasn't that enough?

Suddenly, Luke said goodbye. "I have to go," he said. "I didn't sleep so great. I think I'll go home and take a nap."

Salm looked at him with surprise. "Home? Why don't you just take a nap here? I'll put the air on for you." She was feeling desperate about the impending end of their connection.

Luke examined the palms of his hands and thought about having them read. He couldn't remember which crease represented the life line. "No." His message was firm. "I'll be fine. Thanks. I appreciate it. I want to do some work today anyway. I want to check in on Mitch too."

Salm put some chipperness in her voice. "Well, I'm not doing anything. I'll come with." Luke didn't speak. Salm waited for a response. "OK?"

She got an answer she didn't want. "Look, I'm sorry," Luke told her, "but I want to be by myself today. You know how that is."

"Want to make plans for later?" she asked, still keeping a positive tone. She refused to sound beaten.

"I don't know." He reached down and put his coffee cup on the porch. "I'll call you," he said, as he got up, pushing his hair off his face. He bent down to kiss her on the cheek.

"I love you," she said, forcing a happy lilt in her voice.

He held his fingers to his lips and then gently laid them on hers.

She had never before heard a louder and clearer sense of ending and finality in such a silent action. She listened to the sound of his footsteps fade as he descended the stairs. He was gone and then there was silence. Slowly, the silence itself started climbing through her, a desperate thing that scaled her muscles, up from her legs and into her chest, up through her throat and into her mouth. It was completely inside of her and needed to get out. She wanted to scream and expel it from her body. But no sound would come.

She sat quietly on the glider, rocking back and forth for hours, until complete mental exhaustion set in. She lay down, her arms crossed over her chest. Sleep came quickly, when she least suspected it. She dreamed in slow motion, paralyzed with fear.

In a glistening white room, she was strapped onto an operating table. From behind a glaring silver light, a band saw came down and began to slice her body into even, clean pieces. The first cut began in between her little and fourth toes and the saw buzzed up through her leg, her hip, the side of her arm, her shoulder. Her eyes, opened wide, stared at the surgeon.

"Don't move," he commanded.

She was conscious of what was happening to her, but she followed the orders.

"Don't move," the surgeon said again, as the second slice began.

She nodded.

He placed his latex glove over her forehead. "I told you not to move."

If she awoke, she knew she would find the same thing happening to her in her own bed. If she stayed in the dream, at least she was numb to the pain.

# XXXII

Luke didn't call Salm later that day. Not the next day, or the one after that. Mitch had died.

Barbara, Mitch's sister, called Luke with the news. "Mitch had phoned to say he wasn't feeling well, and that Jack, that's my husband, you remember? That Jack should come over and take him to the hospital." Her voice was hushed and delicate. "And that worried me, you know. Mitch wasn't one for doctors."

"Yeah. I know," Luke said.

"And when Jack got there, he found Mitch sitting in that big chair in the living room, you know the one."

"Yeah." Luke knew. The chair next to the ham radio.

"He was dead, poor man. All alone. We feel so awful about it. It was his heart, Luke. He had been having trouble." Luke didn't know that. Mitch had never told him he was having "trouble."

"Do you know if the radio was on?" Luke asked. He needed to know if Mitch had tried to communicate with him and if he had failed him in any way. Could he have gotten him to the hospital on time or have done anything to make a difference?

"Oh, Luke," Barbara said sympathetically. "Don't think about that. You couldn't have done anything. He was a sick man."

"I need to know."

"Jack?" she called out. Then Luke heard her cover the mouthpiece. She tried to speak quietly but Luke could still hear her. "Luke wants to know about the radio. You know how Mitch used to talk to him through it."

"What about it?" Jack asked her.

She was whispering. "Was Mitch trying to get through to him on the radio? Was it on?"

Luke held his breath during the pause while Jack recounted the scene in his head.

"Nope," he finally said. "No. He was just sitting there. Peaceful-like. He hadn't been doing anything with the radio. He was just sitting there."

At the funeral parlor, Luke struggled to adequately perform the behaviors of the ritual. He moved up to stand near the casket, first in front of it, and then to the left. After that, he stood to the right. He wove his fingers together and cupped them politely over his crotch. He forced both his hands into his back pockets. Then he would dip one hand into a front pocket and toy with his keys. His other hand dangled at his side.

Mitch didn't look comfortable either. His body seemed self-conscious and deliberate, laid out straight and silent in the coppery casket. His face was set into an eerie, stern expression. It was the expression Mitch's face held when the kids in the street made too much noise. It wasn't the expression he had when Luke last saw him. He should have looked kinder.

Luke moved to the rear of the parlor and sat in a tall hardback chair, its wooden slats pushing into his shoulder blades. Salm had a chair in her kitchen that felt like this one. Luke closed his eyes and imagined himself to be there, in Salm's kitchen. He had been missing her, more than he imagined he would. He wanted to touch her hand and hear her speak. He recalled how much he enjoyed just looking at her face.

"Hey." Luke was startled by George's voice. George patted Luke on the shoulder. "Too bad, huh?" George said, nodding toward the casket. "He was a great old guy."

Luke nodded. A sudden roar traveled through him like the roar of his p.a. system gone mad in his brain.

George sat down next to Luke. "He never got to see my kid either."

"I told him about him though."

"Really? Good."

"Yeah. After I left you that day at the hospital, I went over there. Told him I was going to call the kid Thor. Mitch liked it. He thought Thor was better than George, Jr., too. He even said something about how you ought to move back into the neighborhood, with all the yuppies and their kids, or something like that."

George smiled. Then the two of them sat together silently, each recalling their own memories, images, and words while they watched people linger at the casket and talk to Mitch's sister and her husband. It was a small funeral, filled with a few familiar faces from the old neighborhood. Mitch would have been pleased to see them all.

"It's too bad he didn't have any kids, huh?" George said at one point during the memorial service. Both he and Luke were pall bearers. "No kids to mourn you. That's a sad thing."

Luke didn't respond. He was angry at George for saying it. Did George believe that Mitch without kids wasn't as good as Mitch with kids would have been? Hell, what if he *had* had a child? Maybe it would have been the kind of kid who wouldn't have shown up at the funeral at all, the kind who wouldn't give a shit. He had had a good life, that's what Mitch told Luke. That's what was important. He took the life he wanted away with him.

Luke looked down at the casket and suddenly remembered Mitch's smile, how it would come on like lightning, a flash that would light up his whole face, and then disappear just as quickly. Luke recalled his teeth. They were good teeth. Strong, big, white ones.

# XXXIII

"Miss you. Call me," Salm cheerily said into Luke's answering one more time. She had left four messages in the last three days. This message would be the last one. She had thought about being worried about him. Maybe he had become the victim of a random street crime, or had succumbed to a killer flu or killer bee, but she knew better. She had holed herself up in her apartment, hopelessly (she knew) waiting for a call or a surprise visit. But none came.

Her world had changed and she felt hollow. She decided to fashion her own private wake to take her from one phase of her life to the next. "Get over it and go on," her Aunt Elaine would have said.

She went to the liquor store around the corner and stocked up on cabernet and cigarettes. This is how she would begin.

Salm sat on the back porch in her white silk pajamas, the ones reserved for such occasions. They were the pajamas her mother wore on her wedding night, and she wore them again after Salm's father's death. Salm remembered her mother lying on the couch, drinking vodka and orange juice, sometimes sleeping, sometimes staring at the floor while tears traced their patterns on her cheeks. Salm would stroke her mother's forehead and tell her they would be all right. They had been loved.

Now, Salm sat and stroked the white smoothness of the silken fabric. A few months after her father died, Salm spotted the pajamas in a box of things her mother was donating to the Salvation Army. Salm rolled them up into a ball and stuffed them into her hair dryer case. Her mother never knew she had them.

She took a sip of the warm, rich wine and lit a cigarette. She reviewed the relationship file permanently stored in her brain. Ben. Dominick. Alex. Frank. Sachin. Steve. Jonathan. Anthony. Some names connected with faces. Others didn't. Mike. Walter. Edwin. Bill. Charlie. Sal. She would get up and make herself a grilled cheese sandwich, her favorite comfort food.

She slept late, woke up feeling fuzzy and a little shaky. She drank coffee at the kitchen table and inhaled the thick, humid smells that rose from between her legs and from under her arms. She chewed at her cuticles, gnawing and eating her own flesh. She worked for a few hours, still in her white pajamas. After a nap, she lay on the couch. She would claw at the callouses on her feet, pulling off pieces of dead skin, dumping them in a little pile under the coffee table. She played bitter, tragic love songs and sang along, wiping tears from her face, wiping snot on her pajama sleeve. The next day would be the same.

Salm had been through this mourning activity before, a ritual that she suffered through without question. But this time, it was different. She couldn't say to herself things like, "You'll be better off," or "It's just going to take some time." Salm was convinced that Luke was her last chance. She blamed herself for everything. Maybe she wasn't worthy after all.

A phone call from Sylvia inspired her to leave her apartment. Claire was back from Greece, and they were all meeting at The Cup. She took the long way to the diner.

Nick was glad to see all of the women together again.

"How are my beauties?" he asked. They nodded quietly, and moved their heads toward Salm. Nick patted her on the back sympathetically. He easily spotted the wounded. They were a common presence in his all-night diner. While Nick walked away, Salm lit another cigarette. She was up to the part where Luke told her that he would call.

"And then he left. And that was that."

"Oh, you never know. He loved you." Sylvia tried to sound upbeat and convincing.

"Past tense?" Salm asked.

"I didn't mean it that way. He loves you, OK?"

"But c'mon," Salm said. "Love or no love. I'm not what he wants. I'm not what anyone wants."

"Oh, Christ," Sylvia said, "that's going too far. Being pathetic doesn't make it, Salm."

"I know, but I feel like feeling sorry for myself."

"It's not you, Salm," Claire said. Her summer in Greece had left her tan and glowing. "It could be anything."

"Christ, buying the wrong yogurt flavor is usually enough," Wendy joked, trying to lighten up the conversation.

"Call him and tell him you want to talk. He owes you that."

"I've already called him. It's not like he doesn't know where to find me," Salm said. "And I'm not going to beg. I'm not humiliating myself like that."

"It's not humiliating at all. You have to find closure," Claire said.

"Fuck you and your closure." Salm wasn't going to try to camouflage her bitterness.

Wendy reached over the table. "Hand me your lighter."

"What do you think, Wendy?"

"It's typical male crap. Now I love you. Now I don't. Fear. Paranoia. Angst. Bullshit." Wendy flipped open the top of the creamer and checked for curdling. "I'll tell you what though. My son is never going to do anything like that to any woman."

Claire laughed. "So how long do we have to wait til he's eighteen?" The women began rearranging the table, emptying ashtrays, pouring more coffee.

"I feel so sick," Salm whispered, holding her head. "I can't believe what I did to myself."

"You have to stop punishing yourself, Salm. Just wait," Sylvia said. "Give him some time. He'll change his mind. He'll come back."

The women looked around at one another and smiled nervously in unison. Time had never made a difference in their past relationships. Once the distance was there, it never disappeared. No one ever came back. Claire pulled a letter from her purse. "I got something from my fisherman." She waved it under Sylvia's nose and began to read aloud.

Salm periodically found herself passing by Luke's. She knew Luke was home—she had checked the alley and saw his car. Once, she gathered the courage to approach the front door and leave a note on his mailbox saying she was going to visit her mother and stepdad in Arizona and that she and Luke should get together, for coffee or something, when she got back. She tried to make the note sound lighthearted and pleasant. It took her hours to write the one sentence it contained. She imagined he would just throw it away.

She really did go to Arizona and spent a lot of time in a lawn chair in her mom's front yard looking at old family pictures. One morning, her mother came out and sat next to her. "You know, Samantha, I feel bad. I taught you how to iron and how to make good pie crust, but I guess I never taught you how to keep a man." She spoke to her daughter as she pulled wiry curlers from her head. Salm decided to leave that afternoon on the train.

Somewhere in the desert, she made love to a photographer she met in the train's club car. She remembered that her Aunt Elaine had always been a sucker for photographers. She told Salm, "You can't help but be crazy about a man who can capture a moment in time and keep it that way forever."

When the photographer asked if he could call Salm the next time he was in Chicago, she laughed at him. "No," she said. "Don't even think about doing that."

She watched the terrain move past the window and felt her attachment to Luke flourish inside of her, like some kind of spindly cactus whose appendages had grown wild from a dangerous chemical.

Back in Chicago, she spent time inspecting her hands, searching for stigmata. She imagined herself growing older, then old.

# XXXIV

Luke came to prefer candlelight. Amber-colored candles lined up across the bar were as much illumination as he could stand. Constantly, the public address system hummed through bar, permeating the space with a consoling energy, gently washing the air with its hiss. Luke knew that one day he would turn it off, but he wasn't ready, not quite yet.

He finally fixed the dripping faucet behind the bar. Daily, he checked off his tenants' requests—replace the lightbulbs on back landing at the Wabansia building, paint the entrance hall at Bob's, install a new gas line on Carolyn's stove. He often took "Thor" out for a walk in his stroller, even though it made Gail nervous to put her newborn into his hands.

Luke had unscrewed the mannequin arms that Salm had attached to the wall and stacked them onto the corner table where they once were stored. The air in his place still swarmed with Salm's energy. Fuzzy images of her face appeared before him, followed by a remembrance of her malformed finger, beckoning to him.

Sometimes at night, he would push the candles aside and lie on top of the bar, crossing his arms over his chest, and pretend to play dead. He imagined feeling his lips turn blue and envisioned the blackness of his own casket. Who would be there to mourn him? He tried to picture their faces but they were all featureless, except for Salm's. He could see her tears so clearly.

When he slept, he dreamed of Mitch's voice floating over him in waves of blue neon.

"Luke? Luke?"

Luke would snort and grumble, twisting and turning under his sheet.

"You're gonna have some regrets, Luke. No way around that. But you're a lucky sonnofabitch, you know that?"

Luke's eyes would frantically move beneath his closed lids.

Mitch would whisper. "You get to take only one life with you, Luke. Make sure it's the one you want."

Luke would wake in the mornings after these dreams feeling exhausted and lonely. The words haunted him. He didn't know what he wanted. How could he ever choose?

He had read Salm's note, and as she imagined, he crumpled it in his hand and threw it away. Later, though, he dug it out of the garbage and kept it on one of the tables. Sometimes he would stare at the curvy lines the felt pen had made on the paper. He would trace the shapes of the words with his fingertips. He remembered telling her, "We're made for each other, you know."

He went for long, long walks and he played basketball. He drank beers with George.

"God, you love her, don't you?" George asked him once.

Luke didn't answer.

"Don't be an asshole," George said. "Don't fucking throw that away."

# XXXV

As the wet autumn leaves squeaked underfoot, Salm lugged four small pumpkins up the stairs to her apartment. She spread several Sunday papers onto the kitchen floor and sat down, putting the pumpkins between her legs. She cut deep wounds around their stems, and after pulling off the tops, she settled in for the best part of the job—digging her hands into the cold slime and separating the stringy innards from the seeds. She spent the early evening washing the pumpkin seeds, salting them, and baking them in her oven. She was going to take the seeds to Sylvia and Reed's tomorrow. They had just moved in together, and they were having a Day of the Dead celebration in conjunction with their housewarming party. Reed had told her he had a mild addiction to pumpkin seeds. While the seeds cooked, Salm sliced unhappy geometric expressions into the pumpkins' faces.

Sylvia had introduced Salm to the Day of the Dead rituals—Dia de los Muertos—years ago. It was the day the dead came back to visit the earth. Creating an altar with candles was essential. The altar honored their memory, and the candles guided their way.

After the pumpkins were carved, Salm lined them on top of her kitchen table. She went into her pantry and dug out the voodoo candles she bought at Maxwell Street last year—thick, round candles encased in sparkling glass. Her cats followed Salm from room to room as she roamed her apartment, picking up assorted mementos—photographs, bits of memorabilia, postcards, souvenirs, a book of poetry, letters, holy cards. On her bureau, she found Luke's dog magnets. She arranged and rearranged everything until the memories were in their right places. Then she sprinkled the entire creation with glitter. Satisfied with the altar's look, she rummaged through the cabinet under her sink to find an old bottle of mescal and poured herself a double shot. She lit the candles and turned off the overhead light.

She sat at the kitchen table and watched the candles flicker. "To the dead," she began, lifting the shot glass to her eyes and squinting through it. She threw the fiery liquid down her throat.

Salm toasted to the pumpkins. "To Dad." She sighed.

"Aunt Elaine, Grandma and Grandpa Collins, Big Fred, Grandma Penszak." She sat in silence.

"To Sandy, my guardian angel, Bobby Kennedy, Uncle Walt, Theresa, Peter. Jennifer, Cal, Les, Stuart, Rick, Terrence."

As always, Luke was on her mind. "To Luke's parents, his Uncle Jerry, Greg, Anne Marie and all the rest." She felt a certain numbness from the mescal overtaking her fingers and toes.

"To all of the lovers and friends who are dead . . . really dead . . . and the ones who are dead to me from absence." She felt tears burn in her eyes.

"And, of course, to Luke." She spoke quietly and solemnly.

The candle flames quivered and swayed, catching and reflecting the light of the raindrops on the window.

Salm sat still for a long, long time.

She thought she heard a knock at the back door, but it must have been a branch, or a tipped garbage can being blown down the alley.

"It's open," she thought to herself. She remembered saying that to Luke so many times.

There was another knock. She looked up to the back door and thought she saw Luke's image through the screen. She wondered if the mescal could cause such a hallucination.

"Salm?" Luke said quietly. He hadn't realized how much he needed to see her until he saw her features in the candlelight. "Salm," he said again, his forehead pressed against the screen.

She looked away from him and bowed her head to look at her hands. Luke stood still, not sure of what to say or what to do.

"Can I come in?" he asked.

In her head, Salm replied, "It's open." Even though she didn't speak, he had heard her somehow.

He walked in and pulled a chair next to Salm's. He sat so closely to her that their shoulders and thighs touched. He felt Salm's body freeze. She wanted to pull away from the slight contact, but she couldn't. That strange force kept them connected. They both stared straight ahead, watching the candles. Salm's stomach gurgled. The wind blew the screen door open and slammed it shut again.

"Salm?" he asked.

She turned and looked at his profile. He continued to stare at the altar.

Because it was safer, he spoke directly to the orange eyes of the pumpkins. "I don't know everything that I want, Salm. I still can't define that. But I found out there's something I don't want."

He gave in and turned to her.

She wanted to kick him, to tell him to get out. She wanted to bury her head in his shoulder and beg him never to leave.

Luke put his hand on hers. "You know one thing for certain, Salm. You know that you don't want children."

She sighed.

"And I know something for certain. I know that I don't want a life without you in it. I don't want a life apart from yours." He noticed the magnetic dogs on the table and reached out for them. He leaned over and stuck the magnets on the side of her refrigerator. "They stick," he said. He tried to get her to smile. "One of the constants in life, the selections in those vending machines."

Salm tried to suppress a grin and finally spoke. "Yeah, like you always said, you can always count on them being there."

Their eyes moved from the candles to the magnetic dogs on the side of the refrigerator and back again to the candles. "But sometimes it's so hard to pick," Luke said. "You pick the schnauzers maybe, but what you really think you want afterwards is the key chain with the dice. Then you realize that the schnauzers were maybe what you wanted in the first place."

They felt their electrical connection spark, surge, and oscillate.

"And you could stand there and stare at the selections in those vending machines forever and end up never getting anything. But if you want anything, you have to take a chance, you know. You have to pick."

Salm remembered standing next to Luke at the Museum of Science & Industry, as if it were yesterday. She was overwhelmed by the fact that Luke was next to her again. It seemed an eternity since she saw him last. "But how do you ever choose?" she asked.

"I don't know exactly, but I'm going with what's inside of me. And my insides are telling me that my life needs you in it."

They turned and looked at each other, while their eyes spoke in code—apologizing, forgiving, understanding, and wanting.

"Maybe we don't have to create another human being, Salm, but we can create a life together."

They both stopped breathing. "You think?" Salm asked, finally exhaling.

"Yeah," Luke answered. "I think."